'Hang on, hang on …' said Matt, holding his hand up in an attempt to get her to halt.

'Yes?' she said, blinking up at him through her specs.

'Sorry, do I know you?' asked Matt.

'Kitty Hope,' she said, 'I'm eleven years old, I'm serious about management, and comedy is a serious business. You've got real talent, Matt Mills, you could be big and I'd really like to be involved.'

FABER & FABER has published children's books since 1929. Some of our very first publications included *Old Possum's Book of Practical Cats* by T. S. Eliot starring the now world-famous Macavity, and *The Iron Man* by Ted Hughes. Our catalogue at the time said that 'it is by reading such books that children learn the difference between the shoddy and the genuine'. We still believe in the power of reading to transform children's lives.

HARRY HILL

Illustrated by **STEVE MAY**

FABER & FABER

ABOUT THE AUTHOR

Harry Hill is one of the UK's finest and most original stand-up comedians. His unique brand of humour has been rewarded with numerous awards, countless nominations and many accolades.

Born in Woking in 1964, Harry grew up in Kent, then qualified as a doctor. Luckily for us, he decided to focus on his comedy career, and the rest, as they say, is history!

ALSO BY HARRY HILL

A Complete History of Tim (the Tiny Horse)
Harry Hill's Whopping Great Joke Book
Harry Hill's Bumper Book of Bloopers
Harry Hill's Colossal Compendium

ABOUT THE ILLUSTRATOR

Steve May is an animation director and freelance illustrator. Steve was born in 1968 in Hastings and spent his childhood drawing and discovering interesting ways of injuring himself. After studying Fine Art and film-making, Steve completed an MA in Animation. He has illustrated books by Jeremy Strong and Philip Reeve, as well as the Dennis the Menace series.

First published in 2017
by Faber & Faber Limited
Bloomsbury House,
74–77 Great Russell Street,
London WC1B 3DA
This paperback edition first published in 2018

Printed in the UK by CPI Group (UK) Ltd, Croydon, CR0 4YY
Typeset by MRules

A CIP record for this book
is available from the British Library

ISBN 978–0–571–33249–6

2 4 6 8 10 9 7 5 3 1

For My Pal Stanley Baker

1

Defying Gravity

He prowled the stage like a prize fighter, rolling out one-liners in waves. BANG! That was a belter! WHACK! That one was a killer! POW! That one knocked 'em dead on their feet!

The audience were reeling now! Dazed! Their heads were thrown back in laughter! They were out of control! Tears were streaming down their hot, sweaty faces! Snot was bubbling out of their noses! Three of them looked like they were about to choke!

Then – just as the laughter was starting to subside – THWACK! He let rip with another gag – even funnier than the last! SPLAT! BOP! KABOOM!

When he'd first walked out onstage they'd been just a room full of people – now they were a single being, united in their love of his stand-up comedy skills.

'That's all from me – goodnight!' he shouted and was gone.

As he walked off the stage of the mighty Hammersmith Apollo the applause was deafening and Matt Mills, aged just twelve, loved every minute of it.

'They're on their feet, Matt!' gushed the MC as Matt passed him in the wings. 'They want a bit more! You'd better go back on or there'll be a riot!'

Matt rolled his eyes as if taking this kind of adulation from a few thousand people was a daily occurrence.

Then the chanting started.

'More! More! More! We want Matt Mills! We want Matt Mills!'

'Just another day at the office!' said Matt, his face breaking into a big smile. With that he turned a full 180 and walked back out to meet his crowd – to even bigger cheers than before.

Three encores later and Matt found himself at the stage door fighting his way through a barrage of flashes. A huge crowd of paparazzi and excited fans had gathered with cameras and smartphones held aloft.

'Matt! Can I get a selfie?'

'Matt! Will you sign my ticket?'

'Matt! Will you sign my dad's bald head?!'

Girls, boys, men, women, children – people of all ages, sizes and colours were clamouring for a piece of him.

'Matt! I love you!' screamed one old lady clutching a bottle of beer and a felt-tip pen.

'I love me too!' he quipped, to another massive laugh. He couldn't help himself – he was just SO funny!

'You didn't just knock 'em dead, Matt. You buried 'em!' said Matt's manager as he sank back into the plush leather seat of his limo. 'Now we need to talk about the tour.'

'Sure, where do you want to start it?' said Matt, taking a tub of ice cream out of the in-car fridge.

'We start with twelve nights at the O2 Arena, then hit all the major cities in the UK,' said his manager.

'And then?' quizzed Matt.

'We hit the States!'

Matt nodded coolly, flicking on the TV – to see a video of himself outside the Apollo from just ten minutes earlier.

'We interrupt this programme to bring you a newsflash,' said the presenter. 'Matt Mills has just broken the world record for the youngest comedian ever to sell out the Hammersmith Apollo. There were chaotic scenes outside the theatre tonight when Matt was mobbed by thousands of fans all eager to get close to the rising star . . .'

Matt's manager high-fived him.

'Now, there have been a couple of requests . . .' he continued. 'Kanye and Kim are in town and wondered if you fancied going round for a game of Twister? Rihanna's asking whether you'd like to hang out with her backstage at her Wembley gig and maybe go for a pizza after? Oh, and Buckingham Palace called – turns out you're Will and Kate's favourite comedian and they'd like you to do Prince George's birthday party.'

Before Matt could answer, something weird

started happening to his manager's voice. It was changing, changing pitch, sounding younger. 'Matt . . . Matt . . . ? Hello?'

Matt blinked and looked up to see the face of his best mate, Rob Brown, staring at him.

'Hello?'

Matt looked around. He wasn't in the back of a limo, he was in a classroom. It wasn't late at night but broad daylight. Then it dawned on him – he hadn't just done a gig at the Hammersmith Apollo, and he wasn't Britain's youngest stand-up comedian. He was a twelve-year-old boy putting together the jokes page for his school magazine.

'You were daydreaming again, Matt!' said Rob, slapping a picture on to the desk in front of him. It showed their physics teacher falling down the steps outside the science block.

'Oops!' said Matt, confused and more than a little crestfallen.

'We need a caption for this photo of Dr Bouvier,' said Rob.

And like Dr Bouvier, Matt was back down to earth with a bump.

'Um . . .' said Matt, rubbing his eyes and blinking himself back to the here and now. 'How about "Bouvier finally explains gravity in a way that's easy to understand!"?'

'Hmmmm . . .' said Rob, rubbing his chin and desperately trying to come up with something to top Matt's gag.

'Hang on, scratch that, how about "What goes up, must come down!"?'

'Nice one!' said Rob. 'I don't know how you do it, but you always do.'

'Teamwork, Rob, teamwork!' said Matt and they set to planning the rest of the page.

Matt and Rob had been running 'Pavey's Punchlines' for over a year and it had been going really well. Meredith Pavey was their headmaster – a bald man with glasses, a very odd dress sense and a personality to match. In short he was a cartoonist's dream.

'What're you thinking for the main feature, Matt?'

'I thought we might try a cut-out-and-keep, dress-it-yourself model of Pavey in his underpants.'

'Like it, keep talking.'

'You're the artist, Rob. You draw a picture of Pavey in his undies, then around that we'll put some of his most popular outfits with little tabs on so that our readers can cut them out and dress him up for different occasions. We'll give him that dumb green tracksuit he wears on sports day . . .'

'His flasher's mac ...' chipped in Rob.

'The sandals ...' countered Matt.

'The stripy tank top ...'

'Yes, but make sure it's like the real one and doesn't cover his belly button!'

'The flowery tie he wears for assemblies!'

'The Speedos ...' said Matt with a giggle.

'Oh man, stop it!' said Rob, cracking up now. 'We'll get lynched!'

'A bobble hat and a pair of mittens ...'

'What, with the Speedos?'

'Whatever floats your boat, Rob!'

They were really cooking now, bouncing ideas off each other, pushing it further and further until they were virtually rolling around on the floor with laughter.

'Er . . . I hope there's some work being done here!' said a big man with a cauliflower ear and a beard, leaning round the door of the classroom. It was Mr Gillingham, who supervised the school magazine activity. He looked like a real hard case and more than a little scary, but in fact Paul Gillingham had a great sense of humour and was a big fan of Mills and Brown. He'd picked up the mangled ear from one too many games of rugby.

'Oh yes, sir, the joke page is really filling up nicely,' said Matt.

'Yeah? What have you got for us this week?' said Mr G, perching himself like a giant bearded budgie on the edge of Matt's desk. 'Hard to beat last month's School Dinner Bingo.'

That had been another of Matt's ideas – photos of various school dinners placed in boxes in a grid like a bingo card. Readers had to try to match the name of the dish to the photo. It had gone down a storm with pupils and teachers alike, even if it had meant being blanked by the dinner ladies for a week and smaller portions for Matt and Rob from the head cook, Mrs Rogers – mind you, you could call that a blessing in disguise.

'It's a fashion piece,' said Matt, passing Mr Gillingham Rob's rough sketch. A broad grin spread across Mr Gillingham's face as he scanned the page, then he let out a snort and finally a big laugh.

'One day you two are going to get me sacked! You can't stick this in the magazine! Mr Pavey will hit the roof!'

'Oh, sir, please? You've got to admit it's really funny,' said Matt, falling to his knees with his hands clasped together, mock pleading.

'That's true – unofficially. I suppose if a few copies of it were printed anonymously using the school photocopier and circulated amongst friends ... it would be very difficult to level the blame at anyone in particular. Of course you didn't hear that from me.'

'Yes, sir!' said Matt. 'Not hearing you loud and clear!'

'Put me down for ten copies,' chortled Mr Gillingham, heading towards the door. 'Oh!' he said, turning back. 'And don't forget the khaki shorts he wears when the sun's out!'

'With the brown knee-length socks and sandals, sir?'

'You don't miss a trick, do you, Mills?'

'We're on it!' said Rob with a chuckle.

As Mr G left he passed their classmate Ahmed at the door with a bundle of A4 posters under his arm.

'Hello, Ahmed, what are you up to?'

'Mrs McGregor asked me to put these posters up,' said Ahmed with a yawn.

'Ah, the all-powerful drama department. You'd better put them up then. See you later, lads, and remember, mum's the word!'

Ahmed stepped into the classroom. 'Got any Blu-tack, boys?'

'No Blu-tack here, bruv,' said Rob.

'Not seen any round these parts since the great Blu-tack crash of 2014,' joked Matt, affecting a

Texan drawl. 'I heard that lumps of Blu-tack are now changing hands for thousands of pounds and last week a man got mugged for a roll of Sellotape . . .'

'I'm serious, McGregor's told me to put this lot up all round the school by the end of break,' said Ahmed, holding up the stack of posters.

'A new poster? How come they didn't ask me to design it?' said Rob, snatching one from the pile. 'What are they for anyway?'

'They're for some talent show. Can you believe it? A talent show in this poxy corner of the world. I've seen more talent in . . . er . . . um . . .'

'A goldfish bowl?' offered Matt.

'Exactly,' said Ahmed. 'I've seen more talent in a goldfish bowl than in this dump.'

'Present company excepted, Ahmed,' said Rob with a smirk, turning back to the poster. 'Terrible layout, I mean look at that font! Looks like a five-year-old did it. First rule of graphic design – you don't go bold AND underline it . . .'

Matt was already scribbling in his notebook. 'Idea for routine – *The F Factor* – a show based on the hit TV talent show *The T Factor*, only for fish.' He pondered where this might go. He'd found it was pretty easy to think of a wacky idea for a routine, but much harder to write the belting great laugh that should end it.

THE F FACTOR –
TALENT SHOW FOR FISH

Presenters Salmon Bewell, David
Whalemeat, Amanda Flatfish

Auditions in a goldfish bowl

Final – get to play the River
Thames ('You're comin' to London!')

'"Anglebrook's Got Talent"?' said Rob, reading out the legend on one of Ahmed's posters.

'Yeah, they're doing it for Comic Relief,' said Ahmed, rolling his eyes. 'So naff!'

'"Do you have a talent that you've been hiding from the world?"' said Rob, reading on. '"Can you sing like Susan Boyle . . ."'

'There's a few girls here that look like her for sure! Yuk yuk,' sniggered Ahmed.

'"Can you dance like Diversity, tell jokes like Eddie Odillo or get your dog to dance like Pudsey?"' continued Rob. '"If the answer to any of those questions is 'yes' then Anglebrook School's Drama Department needs you!"'

'Whoa!' said Matt, suddenly on his feet, his hands reaching for one of Ahmed's posters. 'Go back a bit . . . !'

'"Can you dance like Diversity . . ."' repeated Rob.

'Not that far back,' said Matt, scanning the poster himself. 'Here it is. "Can you . . . tell jokes like Eddie . . . Odillo!"'

Eddie Odillo hosted the *Stand-up at the Apollo* TV show which showcased the country's best up-and-coming comedians. He was sharp-suited, dead cool and effortlessly funny. He was also Matt's comic hero.

'This is it!' Matt exclaimed, jumping to his feet and waving the poster around his head, unable to contain his excitement. This was the clarion call he'd been waiting for.

'You're thinking of entering, right?' said Rob.

Matt turned to his oldest and dearest friend, put his hand on his shoulder and, raising an eyebrow, let him in on the news.

'No, Rob. You and I are going to form a double act!'

'It'll be lame,' sighed Ahmed and ambled off to the next classroom in search of Blu-tack.

2

Everyone's a Critic

'Rubbish!' said Matt's stepfather, Ian, jabbing his finger at the TV remote control and switching from *Stand-up at the Apollo* to a programme about antiques presented by a man the colour of a satsuma. 'You can't replace the old stars,' he said, reaching into a big bag of cheese and onion crisps and stuffing a handful into his mouth. 'That bloke wouldn't know a good joke if it bit him on the bum!'

Suddenly the smile on Matt's face was gone and he was seething. How dare his stepdad disrespect Eddie Odillo. Eddie Odillo! The whizz-kid of stand-up! Who just three months earlier had won 'Best

Stand-up Comedian' at the British Comedy Awards.

Rubbish indeed! Technically that was a heckle, thought Matt, and if Eddie had been in the room he would have dealt with it with a suitably sarcastic put-down. Matt ran down his mental list of one hundred best heckle put-down lines he'd downloaded and learnt off the internet.

- HECKLER: Someone who shouts out to deliberately disrupt your act. Don't try and reason with a heckler — often he has a high alcohol content!

- HECKLE PUT-DOWNS: Funny reply to the heckler which tells them who's in charge. (Hopefully me!) Ideally humiliating him and stopping him from having another

go. It's good to have at least one
up your sleeve. But remember
it's got to stay true to your
comic persona.

-'GOOD'- EXAMPLES OF
        PUT - DOWNS

'I was the same after
my first pint!'

'Isn't it a shame when
cousins marry?'

'I'm sorry, I don't speak Orc.'

'Sorry, I can't understand what
you're saying... I'm wearing
a moron filter.'

'Excuse me, I'm trying to work
here. How would you like it if I
came to where you work and

shouted at you while you're asking
someone if they want large fries?'

'Look, it's all right to donate your
brain to science, but shouldn't
you have waited till you died?'

FAMOUS COMEDIANS' PUT-DOWNS

- Eddie Izzard: 'Check your joke
with your friend first and if he
thinks it's funny, then give it a try.'

- Arthur Smith: 'Is that your real
face or are you still celebrating
Halloween?'

- John Cooper Clarke: 'Your bus
leaves in ten minutes...
Be under it.'

4

- Ricky Gervais: 'This is a big venue, I can't really get into one-on-ones. In a smaller room I'd still ignore you — shut up!'

(Heckler): 'I don't come here to think.'
- Bill Hicks: 'Well, tell me where you do go and I'll meet you there.'

- Russell Kane: 'Why don't you go into that corner and finish evolving?'

- Rufus Hound (to bar staff): 'Can we get some crayons and a menu for this guy to colour in, please?'

Jack Dee: 'Well, it's a night out for him... and a night off for his family.'

'I was the same after my first pint . . . ?' No, that
was no good, Ian wasn't a drinker . . . how about
'Is that a moustache or have your eyebrows come
down for a drink?' No, Ian had many faults but
a moustache wasn't one of them. 'Hey, why don't
you freeze your teeth and give your tongue a sleigh
ride!' No, Matt wasn't really sure what that one
meant.

'You should take your sense of humour on that
show!' he blurted out.

'Eh?' said Ian.

'Your sense of humour, you should take it on that
antiques show!' continued Matt.

'No, it has to be an actual physical thing. You

know, something like an old clock or a painting,' said Ian matter-of-factly, completely missing the point.

'No, what I mean is your sense of humour is so old it's an antique and you should take it to be valued on that show you're so fond of!' said Matt – this wasn't going quite how he'd planned.

'I'm not sure what you're talking about, mate, sorry! Fancy a crisp?' said Ian, offering him the open bag and letting out a big cheese-and-oniony burp. 'BUUuuuurp! Ooops, sorry, I don't know where that came from!'

Matt rolled his eyes, bit his tongue and headed for the door.

Upstairs in his bedroom, Matt gave his black-rimmed glasses a polish, retrieved his little black book from under his pillow and started writing. 'I'll prove to Ian Woodwood and the whole world how funny I can be. "Anglebrook's Got Talent" today; tomorrow The World! One day that won't be Eddie Odillo up there on the stage of the Apollo, it'll be me!' he thought.

Matt loved jokes. Good ones, bad ones, short ones, long ones, blue ones, clean ones, off-colour ones. He loved shaggy-dog stories, one-liners, gags, puns, knock-knocks, Doctor-Doctors, things crossing the road, things changing lightbulbs, things hiding in fridges – he loved them all.

He loved to hear them, but writing them was quite another matter.

He'd read an interview with Eddie Odillo where he'd said that in the old days comics had writers, and had a shared pool of material, a kind of one-gag-fits-all set-up. They'd done what Eddie had called 'mainstream humour' stuff about women, foreigners and fat people. 'Sexist, racist rubbish' was how Eddie had described it (except he'd used a slightly stronger word than 'rubbish'). Eddie explained that it was important for every comedian to write their own stuff and to find what he called their own 'voice'.

Open with your best gag – first impressions are everything. Finish with your second-best gag — it's the one they'll remember on their way home.

Ideally your last gag will be good enough to make them clap and make the person who booked you RE-book you. (The aim is to get rebooked.)

If it's going badly, get off. If it's going well — get off.

Try to tie up any loose ends at the end.

Running gags: gags that you come back to time and time again, building as you go. Audiences love them. They make you look clever — because you are!

Leave them wanting more. No one ever complained that a show was too short. Don't outstay your welcome.

A comic is like a salesman —
sell your routine.
Confidence is all, don't let the
audience see any weakness or
they'll have you for dinner.

HAVING A COMEDIAN
FOR DINNER!

Never blame the audience. They came hoping to be entertained — it must have been something you did. But you can blame the room, the promoter, the weather, the lights, the sound, the MC, the act before you and pretty much everything else.

Keep going. That's it, just keep going. It's not the funniest comedians that are successful, it's the ones that keep going. Be pushy and annoying and knock on doors. It's not enough to be funny.

'Yeah, but what happens if your voice hasn't broken yet?' thought Matt. 'Hey, that's not a bad idea for a gag,' and he started scribbling.

'I went to the doctor the other day. I said, "Doctor,

Doctor! My voice is breaking." He gave me a prescription – for superglue!'

Nah. That didn't work, too obvious. The whole secret of a joke, Eddie had said in the interview, was that a punchline is basically a surprise. The set-up to the joke draws the audience in, and they're trundling along thinking 'Yes, I understand,' and maybe a few of them are thinking 'Where's this going?' Then whoosh! Suddenly the rug is pulled out from under their feet, they get a big surprise . . . and that makes them laugh.

Here's a classic of the genre:

:Mother:: Jimmy! You'll be late for school!

:Jimmy:: But I hate school! The kids are so mean and violent.

One fight after another, bad language – it's like a jungle!.

Mother: You must go!

Jimmy: Why?

Mother: Because you're the headmaster!

'I wish I'd written that one,' thought Matt.

His phone started buzzing. 'There's got to be a gag about vibrating phones,' thought Matt, fumbling to retrieve it from his trouser pocket. Looking back at him from the touchscreen was Rob.

'Hey, bruv, did you see it?' gushed Rob.

'What?'

'Eddie on *At the Apollo*!'

'Oh man, yeah! Best I've seen him and he looked so cool! I loved the one about texting his girlfriend.'

'Yeah, "How come they don't do emojis of a man's face with acne?"'

'Then he pulled that face that looked like an emoji

of a man with acne! How did he do that?'

'Hey, he's Eddie Odillo, dude! He can do anything.'

They did this a lot. Repeating routines to each other that they'd seen on TV, picking them apart, finishing off each other's punchlines.

'I thought Mark McGinty was so lame, that whiny voice of his and all that stuff about Christmas jumpers, really out of date.'

'Ah, yeah, well, I didn't catch Mark's set . . .'

'I don't blame you.'

'No, Ian turned over to watch *Tanned Bloke in the Attic* or whatever it's called, on Channel 5.'

'Ha! Is that a new one?'

'Huh?'

'*Tanned Bloke in the Attic* – is that part of a new routine?'

'It is now!' said Matt, reaching for his pen.

'Listen, Matt, I've been thinking about your double act idea for the talent show.'

'Great!' said Matt. 'All ideas gratefully received.'

'That's just it . . .' said Rob nervously. 'I'm not sure I'm up for it, bruv.'

'What do you mean?' said Matt.

There was the creak of a floorboard from outside his bedroom – someone was coming up the narrow wooden staircase.

'Uh-oh! Got to go! Ian's on his way. We'll talk about it tomoz!'

There was a cursory knock on the door and moments later Ian was in the room, standing at the end of Matt's bed.

'Did I hear you talking to someone?'

'Me? No, Ian.'

'You haven't got your phone up here then? You know your mum doesn't approve of you spending ages on the net.'

'Phone? Me? Up here? No, Ian.'

'Look, Matthew . . .'

Matt cringed. Ian had been in his life for three years and yet still hadn't worked out that he hated being called by his full name. Matthew? Who ever heard of a stand-up comedian called Matthew?

'It's Matt.'

'Of course ... Matt,' said Ian. 'Now, we both know that I'm married to your mother, and since your father hasn't been in touch for a while ...'

Ouch, that hurt but it was true. Matt's dad hadn't been in touch for eighteen months – well, eighteen months and three days to be precise. Matt liked to think that he was working for MI6 on an important top-secret mission abroad but the truth was slightly less exciting. Matt's dad had run off with his personal assistant to the Isle of Wight. He'd received the odd text message, three postcards of a lighthouse, a test tube full of different-coloured sand and a birthday card with sixty quid in it, but apart from that Ian was right. It was just Mum and Ian.

His mum, Jenny, was a well-known dog trainer – and not just any dogs, miniature wire-haired dachshunds. That's tiny hairy sausage dogs to the uninitiated. She ran dog-training classes from home,

had made several appearances on television and was something of a local celebrity. Once a year she'd take a troupe of five of her best dogs up to Birmingham to the national dog show, Crufts, where they'd perform as 'The Dachshund Five', doing routines to chart hits. Although it was work it was a bit of a social too. She'd spend a few days acclimatising the dogs to the Midlands accent before the show and she'd always take a couple of days at the end to 'catch up on business'. Catching up on business was how she had met Ian, who shared her passion for the little critters. Either way, in total she was usually gone for three weeks.

Three whole weeks of being looked after solely by Ian.

He wasn't the handiest man in the kitchen. He didn't use a timer to tell him when the food was ready – he used a smoke alarm. His gravy was so thick you had to slice it. There was a good side though – at least it had solved the problem of the dogs begging for food at the table!

??? COOKING GAGS

My stepdad makes soup so thick that when I'm stirring it the room goes round!

I'll never forget the first time my stepdad made some rock cakes. He passed them round and told me to take my pick. I didn't need a pick, I needed a hammer and chisel!

My stepdad just bought a new juicer and he's trying it out on everything. Have you ever tried toast juice?

It took my stepdad three hours yesterday to stuff the turkey!

was so angry at the end I
could have killed it!

MM Mmm m, my stepdad's
chicken really tickles the palate - he
leaves the feathers on!

My stepdad cooks for fun —
if we're hungry we eat out!

My stepdad feeds me so much
fish I started breathing
through my cheeks!

What do you call someone who
has eaten round at my stepdad's
house? An ambulance!

Did you hear about the chef
who got an electric shock? Yeah, he
stood on a bun and a currant
shot up his leg!

My stepdad's shortbread melts in your mouth. OK, it may take a day or two but eventually it melts in your mouth!

It was taking ages for my stepdad to make a chocolate chip cookie. It didn't take long to make the dough, just ages to peel the Smarties!

So Mum would spend the week before the trip cooking and freezing three weeks' worth of dinners, which she'd then put in the freezer. All Ian had to do was take the Tupperware container out of the freezer in the morning to thaw it out and stick it in the oven in the evening. Simple, right? Nine times out of ten he couldn't even manage that. A couple of times Matt had bitten into his dinner only to find it still frozen in the centre. 'Like a chicken ice lolly!' he'd scribbled in his little black book. That was Ian's one saving grace – he was a brilliant source of comedy material.

'I am, to all intents and purposes, acting in loco parentis ...' Ian continued.

'What's this got to do with a tropical insect?' said Matt with a smirk.

'Eh?' said Ian, confused.

'You said "praying mantis",' said Matt.

'Not praying mantis! Loco parentis – I'm standing in for Dave – your dad.'

'What about when you're sitting down?' asked Matt.

'I'm standing in for him even when I'm sitting down!' said Ian, losing it a bit. 'Listen, Matt, I'm not going anywhere . . .'

'Well, perhaps you should ask your manager for a promotion then!' said Matt. Ian worked in a local estate agent's office, and it appeared to Matt he certainly wasn't going anywhere fast.

'I don't mean like that!' snapped Ian, sharply. 'I'm just saying you've sort of got to treat me a bit more like your dad, with a bit more . . . respect.'

'Sure, no problem . . . Yeeark!' shrieked Matt, suddenly jerking his tummy into the air.

'Are you OK?'

'Fine, ha haaaaaa – oooh!' he replied, twisting back the other way.

It was his phone. He'd shoved it under his armpit to hide it when Ian walked in and now someone was trying to call and the vibrations were tickling him.

'Ooooh haha ahahahaa!'

'What's so funny?!' said Ian.

'Nothing! Hooo haha ha heeeheheheee!!'

'I really wish you'd take this seriously!' moaned Ian. 'Not everything is a comedy sketch!'

'Aha ha heee heee hooo hoooo!' Matt was now writhing about in his bed like a disco-dancing snake at a Taylor Swift concert (it's mainly pythons that like Taylor; cobras tend to go more for hip-hop and anacondas are really into classical music), all the time thinking: 'Please, whoever's calling, just leave a message or hang up!'

At long last the phone's vibrations ceased and calm descended once more upon Matt's tiny frame.

'Sorry, Ian!' he said, slumping flat on the bed. Then he had a thought he just couldn't resist. 'Oh, and Ian?'

Ian turned in the doorway to face him.

'What now?' he moaned.

'That's all from me – goodnight!' grinned Matt.

Ian rolled his eyes and went back down the stairs to the kitchen.

3

You've Got to Be in It to Win It

The next day the whole playground was buzzing about the Mr Pavey cut-out-and-keep doll. It hadn't taken long for a copy to fall into Mr Pavey's hands and the word was that he'd really gone off the deep end. Apparently he'd been so angry that he'd whacked Mr Gillingham a couple of times over the head with a rolled-up copy of it. Luckily Mr G hadn't spilled the beans over who was responsible. The good news was it was already having an effect on the hapless headmaster's dress sense because although the sun was shining there was no sign of those legendary khaki shorts. No, on the day after his complete wardrobe had been well and truly trashed by Mills and Brown Mr Pavey had last been seen heading into Stonebridge Wells to the men's department of Marks & Spencer.

It was now virtually impossible to get hold of a copy of 'Mr Pavey – What Not to Wear', as Rob and Matt had titled it. Most had been confiscated but a few surviving dog-eared copies were being passed around under desks at lessons and someone had even made a copy of a copy and circulated that. For about three hours it had also hit the school's Facebook page, until Mr Curtis in IT had worked out how to take it down.

'It was you, wasn't it, Mills?' said Dave Joy from behind his sunglasses. Dave was four years above Matt and widely considered to be the coolest kid in the school. He had a moustache and a motorbike and a special dispensation to wear sunglasses in lessons (something to do with oversensitivity to light, although the optician who'd signed the letter also happened to be Dave's uncle). Dave could also regularly be seen with his arm around school heartthrob Magda Avery.

'I couldn't possibly comment,' said Matt.

'Yeah, well, it's funny, you're a funny kid,' said Dave in a rare moment of generosity. 'You should enter this talent show. I'm gonna be singing with my band,' he added. Yes, as if Dave wasn't cool enough already he was also the drummer with school band Toxic Cabbage.

'Well, it's funny you should say that . . .' said Matt with a wry smile, 'but me and Rob are going to form a comedy double act.'

'I'm going to be singing "Someone like You" by Adele,' came a girl's voice from over Matt's shoulder.

Matt turned and there she was, Magda Avery – a vision in beautiful blond hair, blue eyes and button nose. Magda Avery, the PE teacher's daughter, full-time heartbreaker and all-round goddess. She took her position at Dave's side and he slipped his arm around her waist. Matt had to admit they looked great together – like Kanye and Kim, like Brad and Angelina before they split up.

'Dagda!' said Matt.

'Eh?' said Dave.

'Like Brad and Angelina became Brangelina, your names combined would be Dagda!' said Matt.

'Don't be sarky,' said Dave with a sneer.

DAGDA

'My mum's lending me an Adele wig from the salon so all I've got to do is learn the words,' chirped Magda, changing the subject and inadvertently letting Matt off the hook.

'You'll be brilliant, darlin',' said Dave, giving her a squeeze.

'GSOH is one of the most popular things that people look for in a partner, it always comes up on dating websites,' said Magda knowledgeably.

'GS oh what?' said Dave, raising one end of his monobrow quizzically.

'Good Sense of Humour!' said Magda and Matt at the same time.

'What do you know about dating websites?' said Dave with a frown.

'Nuffing,' said Magda, defensively. 'Funny guys are attractive, that's all.'

She fixed Matt with a look that turned his legs to jelly. Was she flirting with him? She was Dave Joy's girl! Dave could make mincemeat of him with one twirl of his moustache or a single flex of his monobrow.

'Come on, Mags, let's go down Greggs and get us a couple of sausage rolls,' said Dave.

'No, I wanna stay here and talk some more with Matt,' she said, transferring her arm from around Dave's waist to around Matt's and then leaning down to plant a big kiss on his forehead.

'He'll have to fight me first!' spat Dave, putting his fists up.

'Listen, Dave, let's fight with jokes,' said Matt. 'I'll start. My dad used to say, "Always fight fire with fire," and that's why he was thrown out of the fire brigade!'

Magda let out a huge laugh. Matt looked at Dave. He was floundering, 'Um ... I ... did you hear the one about ...'

'The one about what, Dave?' said Matt.

'Er ... Knock! Knock!' spluttered Dave.

'Who's there?' said Matt.

'Er ... Dave Joy!' said Dave. Matt had him on the ropes and he knew it.

'Hey, Dave. What goes ninety-nine thump?'

'Er . . . a centipede with a wooden leg?'

'No!' said Matt, going in for the kill. 'An ice-cream man being mugged!'

Dave staggered back, reeling from Matt's razor-sharp wit.

'Admit it, you can't top that, you're beat. Magda's made her choice, she's with me now!'

With that Matt took Magda's hand and they walked off together to Greggs, where they both had a jumbo sausage roll and lived happily ever after.

Only that's not quite what happened.

'Come on, Mags, let's go down Greggs and get us a couple of sausage rolls,' said Dave, turning and walking towards the school gate. Magda turned too and they left without so much as a backwards glance.

But the seed had been planted in Matt's brain.

'Funny guys are attractive,' that's what she'd said, this vision from Planet Gorgeous, and it gave Matt something quite simple and pure to take hold of – hope!

He pulled out his iPhone and dialled up Rob.

'Rob? It's Matt!'

'I know, bruv, a picture of you comes up on my phone when you ring, along with your name, "MATT",' said Rob pedantically.

'This is important,' said Matt.

The seriousness of Matt's tone unsettled Rob. 'Uh-oh! Is it the cut-out-and-keep Pavey doll? He's sussed out it was us, hasn't he? My mum's gonna kill me if I get in trouble again.'

'No, listen,' said Matt, cutting Rob off in mid-flow. 'This talent show, we need to win it! I'll see you in Greggs in two minutes.'

Matt hung up. He could just see the top of Magda's blond hair disappearing behind the school's tall perimeter fence and a steely look settled across his face. He wanted fame and he wanted love – and not necessarily in that order.

4

The Jumbo Sausage Roll of Death

'I'm too excited to eat!' said Matt as they got to the front of the queue at Greggs. He scanned around the cafe to see if he could get a glimpse of the goddess, but she'd clearly gone.

'I'll just have a Coke please, Mavis!' he said to the lady behind the counter. 'Want anything, Rob?' but Rob seemed to be staring at his feet.

'I'm feeling sick to my stomach just thinking about standing up in front of a room full of strangers!' he whined.

'Two glasses please, Mavis! Don't be ridiculous, Rob, you'll be fine. I'll be there with you, and besides, they won't all be strangers – you'll know a lot of them.'

'That makes it worse!' cried Rob.

'Just calm it,' said Matt.

'But we don't have any jokes. P'raps we should call it off and concentrate on the jokes page?' said Rob as they sat on a couple of high stools by the window, looking out over Anglebrook's busy high street.

'That's where you're wrong!' said Matt, producing his little black book from the inside pocket of his blazer.

'What's that?' said Rob.

'This . . .' said Matt, pouring them each a glass

of Coke, 'is comedy dynamite! Come on, let's get to work!'

With that Matt started looking for the sort of gags that could be opened up into double act routines. Meanwhile Rob gazed out of the window, an ever-increasing feeling of panic rising up inside him. Sure, he liked putting the jokes page together – although, to be honest, most of the jokes were Matt's. He was more interested in drawing his cartoons and illustrations and in the design and layout of the page. They bounced ideas off each other but Rob was in little doubt that Matt was the driving force. And yes, he liked making people laugh, he loved the feedback in the playground when they'd done a good page – like this Pavey cut-out doll. He liked watching stand-ups on TV, but actually doing it himself? No, that was not something Rob had ever, *ever* really contemplated. He was pretty certain he wanted to become an illustrator or graphic designer. Everyone knew he was the best at drawing in the school and his teachers were confident his next step would be a place at an art school, ideally one in 'the Big Smoke' – London. If this talent show had been about showing off your art skills, Rob wouldn't have felt the slightest bit nervous – but stand-up comedy? He looked over at Matt, his head buried in his little black book of 'dynamite'.

'How about this?' said Matt, scribbling in the back of his physics exercise book. 'You come on with a really fancy hat. I say, "Don't you hate it when you meet a really persuasive hat salesman?"'

'Not sure,' said Rob. In his current state of mind he was finding it very hard to see the humour in anything.

'Well you're not much help! Wait a minute, hang on!' Matt said, pouncing on a scribbled note on one of the pages. He slammed his hand down hard on the table. 'I've got it! This really is the one! "How to cook your sister's boy-band doll!"'

'Eh?' This was classic Matt, thought Rob: just as he was trying to back out of something, here was Matt drawing him back in with his enthusiasm – it was contagious.

'It's a slam-dunk, this one. We come on as a couple of TV chefs, only our recipe is how to cook one of those boy-band dolls . . .'

'Like the One Direction dolls my sister's got?'

'That's it! How to Cook Your Sister's Old Harry Styles Doll! We go through the whole thing – we take its clothes off . . .'

'Ooo-er!' chuckled Rob.

'Roll in flour – then dust yourself off . . .'

'Nice!'

'Place in the oven at gas mark five – then, and here's the punchline, we swap the doll for a cooked chicken and say yes, it does tend to swell up – but so would you if you didn't have a hole in your bum!'

The two of them dissolved into gales of laughter. 'We'll never get away with that last bit!' laughed Rob.

'Doesn't matter – it's the last thing we say anyway, so they can't stop us 'cos we've already stopped!'

'Genius! That is genius!'

'Genius, eh?' said a high-pitched nasal whine behind them. 'Well, perhaps you two geniuses would like to get your massive brains round to my office and explain this!' A skinny hand slapped a copy of the cut-out Pavey doll on to the table in front of them. Their eyes followed the hand up to the face that it belonged to, but they didn't really need to, they'd have known that voice anywhere – it was Mr Pavey.

5

Meredith's Revenge

'Explain yourselves!' barked Pavey, leaning in to Matt and Rob's faces in turn, a big vein on the side of his bald head pulsating like a light show at a cheap disco.

'Any minute that's going to burst and all of us will drown,' thought Matt. They both caught a whiff of the pungent aroma of his cheap pine aftershave. 'He smells like an air freshener!' thought Matt, and as Mr Pavey continued to lecture them on their lack of respect for their elders, Matt's mind wandered into what he hoped might be a promising new comedy routine about short-sighted people and air fresheners.

'Air fresheners must be very confusing for the partially sighted, mustn't they? They open a door, sniff sniff! Oh! A pine forest? I thought this was the loo! Sniff! Sniff! Suntan lotion? I thought I was eating a coconut!' He was no longer in the headmaster's office but behind the microphone, bathing in the warm glow of the spotlight at a packed comedy club.

He imagined the waves of laughter that would roll out from the crowd. 'Hey, have you seen that spray that is supposed to make your old banger smell like a new car? It's a great way to get a good price for your clapped-out second-hand car from a blind person! "Yeah, mate, it's a brand-new car – honest! Yeah, smell it! Brand new!" And I know what you're thinking – what would a blind person want with a car in the first place? Well, maybe it was a gift. All you've got to worry about is the guide dog letting him know it's a rip-off!'

Matt started acting like he was a guide dog trying to let its owner know that he was buying a dud car.

He was down on all fours making whining noises, affecting a Scooby Doo-style voice and pawing at his imaginary master, and the audience were lapping it up.

'Woof! Woof!' he barked, getting angry as he imagined his partially sighted owner closing the deal, and then pretended to bite the vendor's leg. The audience were in stitches. Matt started acting like he was the vendor being attacked by the dog.

The dog seemed so real to him he could almost smell its breath ... wait ... that wasn't a dog, it was Mr Pavey's hot eggy breath on his face, and suddenly he was back in the headmaster's office.

'Well?' snapped Pavey, an inch from Matt's face. 'What have you got to say in your defence?'

He glanced over at Rob, who looked like he was about to start crying. Then a thought struck him.

'Did you know, sir, that a GSOH is one of the most attractive personality traits to the opposite sex?'

'A what-what-what?' spluttered Mr P.

'GSOH – Good Sense of Humour. It's one of the

things that girls and ... er ... women ...' he said with a knowing smile, 'find extremely attractive in a man.'

'What's your point, Mills?'

'Well, this was just a bit of fun, no offence meant, but anyone who is seen to be able to laugh at themselves automatically becomes more attractive to the ladies ... and I guess to the female members of his or her staff.'

Mr Pavey sat back in his chair, seeming to consider this.

'You know,' Matt hammered his point home, 'if a joke had been made about a certain person and then that person was seen to laugh at that joke it automatically would make them more attractive to the opposite sex ...'

'Hm!' Pavey scratched his chin. 'Well, it was fairly amusing I suppose. Yes, and Miss Lassiter, the head of geography, was particularly tickled.' Mr Pavey was smiling now.

'There you go then,' said Matt. 'I'm sure you got

a lot of pleasure out of tickling Miss Lassiter.' He nudged Rob in the ribs.

'Yes. I mean no! I mean ... well ... I ... er. She's a very strong woman, is Miss Lassiter, mentally and I imagine physically. Ahem ... More attractive you say?' He had turned and was now staring at his own reflection in a glass bookcase.

'Can we go now, sir?' said Matt.

'Well, on this occasion I think we might let the matter rest there ...'

'Very sensible, sir,' said Matt. He grinned across at Rob, whose tears had been sucked back up into his eyes. 'If you really wanted to demonstrate what a good sense of humour you've got, we could always print up some more cut-outs, Mr P?'

'Don't push it,' hissed Rob with a scowl.

Mr Pavey hesitated, clearly confused. 'Um ... well ... I'm not ... er ... that is to say ...' There was a long pause. 'I suppose we *could* get a few more copies printed up, just for me and a few ... um ... colleagues ...'

'Right you are, sir!' said Matt. 'We'll need some money.'

'I beg your pardon?' Pavey turned to face them. The vein on his head looked like it might be about to fill back up again.

'To pay for the printing, sir! A fiver should cover it,' said Matt, holding out his hand expectantly.

Rob took a deep breath.

'Oh! Yes, of course,' said Mr Pavey, reaching into his spanking new M&S casual trousers and producing a £10 note. 'Do you have change for a—'

'Call it a tenner!' said Matt, snatching the note from his hand and heading for the door. 'Will that be all, sir?'

'Er ... yes, yes,' said Mr Pavey, turning back to look in the mirror. 'Thank you, boys, and good luck!'

'Pleasure doing business with you!' muttered Matt and shut the door to the headmaster's office behind him.

'How did you manage that?' gasped Rob as they rounded the corner. 'He went from being about to expel us to thanking us for our work and ordering a reprint!'

'Don't forget the tenner!' shouted Matt.

'Matt Mills, you are a legend!'

'It's the all-conquering power of humour, Rob,' he said as they high-fived and ran out of the school building into the sunshine.

'I'll write up the script tonight! See you tomorrow in Greggs! Oh and Rob?'

'Yes, Matt?'

Matt waved the £10 note under Rob's nose.

'The jumbo sausage rolls are on Mr P!'

6

A Cup in the Hand Is Worth
Two on the Head

'It's just a first draft,' said Matt, handing Rob three sides of A4 paper. 'You know we can expand it with ad libs . . .'

'Ad whats?' said Rob.

'Ad libs – you know, where you make stuff up as you go along.'

KEY COMEDY TERMS
Ad lib: An off-the-cuff remark.

Some of the best ad libs were written months in advance! So often audiences think the comedian is 'making it up as you go along'. Don't take this as an insult. This is the ultimate compliment. It means you hooked them in and they forgot they were watching an act.

Improvisation: Reacting to something that's happened in the room off-the-cuff is a great skill to develop. Audiences love it because they feel they're getting a one-off, bespoke show that no one else is getting. It also helps

you find other funny stuff within
your existing routines and helps
to build up the act. A little goes
a long way though. Endless working
of the crowd can get pretty
tiresome. This is also called
working the room.

EXAMPLES

'Hey, the pollution is so bad round
here my lungs are having to chew
the air! The pollution's so thick
I shot an arrow into the air
and it stayed there! You have to
put the air in a blender before
you can breathe it!'

'Hey, this is such a rough area — the sort of place you park and RUN!!'

Catchphrases: A catchphrase is a phrase or expression recognised because it's repeated. They become identified with the person whose catchphrase it is and sometimes are enough to get a laugh on their own. They're worth their weight in gold, but here's the bad news — you can't predict the ones that are going to catch on. It's pot luck!

Examples:
'Nice to see you, to see you nice!'
- Bruce Forsyth

'Is it cos I is black?' - Ali G

'Am I bovverred' - Catherine Tate.

'Yeah but no but...' - Matt Lucas.

'Here's another nice mess you've
gotten me into.' - Laurel and
Hardy.

'Just like that.' - Tommy Cooper.

'Bang tidy.' - Keith Lemon.

'You wouldn't let it lie.' -
Vic Reeves & Bob Mortimer.

They were sitting side by side in their usual spot on the bench outside the science block in first break.

'Ha! That's sweet,' said Rob, reading it through. 'I like that bit!'

'Which?' said Matt, leaning over Rob's shoulder, desperate to see which jokes had landed.

'The bit about the Harry Styles doll being reared one better than free range – which means it gets its own room and access to Sky Sports – neat!'

'Yeah, have you got to the bit where . . . ?'

'Ha! Just got to it. This is really funny, Matt. Lots of big laughs, I can just hear you saying it.'

'*Us* saying it, you mean?'

'Sorry, yes, us.' Rob was still very anxious about the whole talent show escapade.

'Mind if I join you, bruvs?' It was Ahmed. 'Is it true about Pavey?'

'Depends what you heard,' said Matt.

'I heard that he paid you fifty quid not to print any more of those cut-out dolls of him you did in the mag.'

'Not exactly,' said Rob. 'He paid us to print more!'

'Yeah, that's right,' interrupted Matt. 'Fifty quid he paid us – so a nice little payday for Mills and Brown!'

'You're kidding me!' said Ahmed.

'Nope. You heard right,' said Matt.

'You jammy little . . .'

'Not jam, Ahmed, hard cash! And plenty more to come when we hit the big time.'

'Oh right, you're still going ahead with this double act idea then,' said Ahmed.

'Yes we are, and we'll need a look,' said Matt, turning to Rob.

'I heard Andrea Morris in year five is doing a dance dressed as a chicken. That's the sort of standard you're up against.'

'A look?' said Rob, ignoring Ahmed's interjection.

'Yeah, something to make us stand out . . . you know, like Tommy Cooper and his fez . . .'

'Who?' said Rob.

'Oh come on, Rob, Tommy Cooper!'

'Has he been on *At the Apollo*?'

'I doubt it, he's been dead for over thirty years,' said Matt.

'Like you are gonna die when you get out in front of that crowd, jus' sayin'!' said Ahmed, grinning.

'Tommy Cooper!' said Matt, ploughing on. 'Ian's always going on about him, and to be fair he had some great gags.'

TOMMY COOPER

TOMMY COOPER 1921 – 1984
COMEDY MAGIC

Best gags:

I said: 'How long will my spaghetti be?' The waiter said: 'I don't know. We never measure it.'

I met my wife at a dance. I thought she was at home with the kids.

Last night I slept like a log. I woke up in the fireplace.

I sleep like a baby. Every morning I wake up screaming around two o'clock.

Matt sprang to his feet, took an empty coffee cup out of the litter bin and upturned it on his head like a fez. He then faced Rob and Ahmed and launched into his best Tommy Cooper impression.

'This bloke goes into a doctor's. He says, "Doctor, I keep thinking I'm a dog!" And the doctor says, "OK, just lie on the couch." And the bloke says, 'Oh no – I'm not allowed on the furniture! Ha ha ha!" Or "Last night I dreamt I was eating a ten-pound marshmallow. When I woke up, my pillow was gone!" Another?'

Rob was really laughing.

'You don't have a choice,' said Ahmed, who was trying hard not to laugh.

'No you don't, it's the comedy rule of three,' said Matt.

'Rule of three?'

'You mean you don't know about the rule of three? Rob Brown, you have got so much to learn.'

'Tell me about it! And we've only got a week.'

'You gonna die, bruv!' laughed Ahmed.

RULES OF COMEDY

1. Go anywhere, any time, any place for a gig when you're starting out. The most important thing at that point is stage time. Walk through the snow to Birmingham for ten minutes of laughs and it will be worth it.

2. Watch other comics at work — the good ones to see what they're doing right and the bad ones to see what to avoid.

3. Have fun. Never forget why you got into it in the first place — because it's the most exciting thing you can do on your own in front of a group of strangers. Never let anyone make you feel like it's work. You're

a comedian, you escaped, everyone else works.

4. Be rigorous - try to do
something no one else is doing.
That's impossible, of course, but
with a bit of work you can
make it look like that.

5. Don't be afraid to involve
the audience. They love audience
participation because it feels
live and it's peculiar to a live
show. They also like the idea
that it's someone else being
picked on and not them.

'Four days actually. So I'm in this restaurant,'
continued Matt, 'and I said to the waiter, "Bring
me a chicken." So he brought me a chicken. I said,

"Just a minute, it's only got one leg." "It's been in a fight," he said. I said, "Well, bring me the winner. Ha ha! Just like that!" Mr Tommy Cooper, ladies and gentlemen!' said Matt, taking a bow.

Rob clapped wildly. 'More! More!' he cheered.

'Less! Less!' sang Ahmed, although by the end he'd been laughing as hard as Rob.

'Thank you very much! Thank you!' joked Matt, hamming it up.

'What have you got that cup on your head for?' came a voice behind him: the goddess Magda Avery.

'Um, oh . . . er . . .' Matt stuttered, his confidence suddenly sucked out of him. 'I was just explaining who Tommy Cooper was.' He could feel a trickle of something cold and wet running down his forehead.

'Tommy who? Is he on *Eastenders*?' said Magda.

'No, he is not on *Eastenders*, he's . . .'

'He's some dead guy with a cup on his head,' said Ahmed.

The cold wet feeling had travelled over Matt's left

eyebrow and under his glasses and he could now feel the ticklish sensation of a drip forming on the end of his nose. He stuck his tongue out just in time to catch a drop of cold coffee.

'Mmmm, I love a coffee break, don't you?' he said, taking the paper cup off his head. 'I find that turning the cup upside down on your head is the only way you can get every last drop out!'

Magda looked at him as if he was completely mad, Ahmed rolled his eyes and Rob chuckled.

'OK, so, Matt, is it true you got two hundred quid off Mr Pavey for working as his personal stylist?' said Magda, eyes wide in wonder.

'Yes – well, no,' said Matt. This whole Chinese whispers thing was getting out of hand.

'How's your Adele coming along?' said Rob, stepping in to change the subject.

'My Adele?' said Magda. 'Oh yeah, it's going really well. I've sorted out a wig – you know my mum works in a hairdresser's – and I've found out what make-up Adele wears . . .'

'What about the actual singing though?' said Matt. 'That's quite an important part, I would have thought.'

'I'm getting to that, silly,' said Magda giving him a playful push. 'I've downloaded the track and the lyrics and Dave is helping me practise.'

'I bet he is,' thought Matt.

'But he's quite busy with his athletics training and of course his band are entering the show, so . . .'

'I could help you!' piped up Matt. He couldn't believe he'd just said it. Rob let out an audible gasp. Ahmed stepped back in amazement.

'You? What do you know about singin'?' said Magda, looking puzzled.

'Well, you know, I could hold your music or teach you the best way to sell a song, you know, eyes and teeth and that . . .' Matt trailed off. He could see the hulking great figure of Dave Joy striding across the playground towards them.

'You?' said Magda.

'You what?' said Dave gruffly, catching them up.

'Oh hello, Dave,' said Magda, throwing her arms around him and giving him a kiss. 'Matt was just offering to help me with my performance, you know, for the talent show.'

'Oh he was, was he?' said Dave, stepping up to Matt, puffing out his chest and towering over him – he was a good foot taller and smelled of sweat and sport and hair gel.

'Nothing formal about it, just a few pointers, eyes and teeth and . . . um . . . posture . . .' stuttered Matt, backtracking like mad.

'I don't think that's a good idea, do you?' said Dave, leaning in, in a rather threatening manner. 'He's the competition, he might be trying to set you up.'

'Well,' said Matt, 'if you're not careful I'll give you two black eyes and ram your teeth down the back of your throat!' and with that he gave Dave Joy a sharp push back, causing him to tumble down the lab steps just as Dr Bouvier had done a few days earlier.

'I'm looking after Magda's singing career from now on!' said Matt, darting down the steps and standing astride the terrified athlete. Then he pulled out his smartphone and started snapping shots of Dave writhing about like a tortoise stuck on its back. 'So if you want to take her to Greggs or anywhere else, you see me about making an appointment first, or these photos find their way on to Facebook! Is that clear?'

(At least, in the daydream Matt had on the bus home that's what happened.)

'What's that?' said Dave, leaning even closer to Matt's face and taking a couple of deep sniffs. 'Eugh! You've got coffee running down your face, you weirdo. You comin', Maggie?'

'S'pose so,' she said, pulling an apologetic face at Matt and setting off in Dave's slipstream.

'That was nicely handled,' said Rob sarcastically.

'So lame,' muttered Ahmed under his breath.

'I'm getting to her. I'm worming my way into her affections,' said Matt, following Magda with his eyes as she headed for the school gate.

'Yeah, worming's about right!' said Ahmed.

'That's a very negative attitude you've got there, Ahmed, and it's really not helping,' said Matt.

'It's not me who's negative, bruv, you seen the face on your comedy partner here?' said Ahmed, pointing to Rob. 'He looks like he's just seen a ghost!'

Matt had to admit Rob did look a bit peaky.

'What's up, Rob?'

'It's just dawned on me we are actually going to be standing up in front of the whole school telling jokes!' said Rob with a gulp.

'Hey, look on the bright side, Rob,' said Ahmed, getting up. 'At least you're not doing it dressed as a chicken! I'll see you two jokers around.'

'See you later, Ahmed, and thanks for your support,' said Matt, turning to Rob. 'Now where were we?'

'We were discussing our new look,' said Rob. 'And as much as I like the brown stripe of dried coffee down the face, I'm not sure it's going to get us booked at the Apollo!'

Matt started laughing. 'That was priceless!'

'Brrrrrrrrrrrrrrring!' The bell rang out loudly across the playground. Break was over and the kids and teachers all started shifting reluctantly towards the various buildings and back to work. School would be great if it was just one long break, thought Matt. It was such a shame that lessons had to get in the way.

'What you got next?' asked Rob.

'Double maths, worst luck,' said Matt.

'Yes! Double art!' countered Rob, punching the air with his fist. 'Result!'

'We'll nip into town at lunchtime, have a look in the charity shops and see if we can't come up with a couple of cut-price outfits,' said Matt. 'Let's get to work!' they said in unison and the two friends went their separate ways.

7

Top of the Pit

That evening on the bus home Matt sat with a carrier bag on his lap containing Mills and Brown's 'new look'. After much umm-ing and ah-ing they'd settled on white shirts and black ties, black skinny jeans and Dr Marten boots.

As the Kent countryside zipped past the window he closed his eyes and started daydreaming about playing the late show at London's legendary Comedy Pit and hanging out with all his favourite comics backstage. Jo Brand, Sean Lock, Sara Pascoe, Jimmy Carr, all sat in the cramped dressing room chatting about who'd done what and where, how long they'd been on for, what gag they'd closed with and who'd bombed.

In his mind's eye Matt saw the dressing-room door open to reveal everyone's favourite glamorous comedian, Eddie Izzard.

'Hi, Eddie! How's the tour going?' said Jo Brand.

'OK, but I need a great opener like Matt Mills,' replied Eddie, adjusting his lipstick in the dressing-room mirror.

'Oh, the goldfish-bowl routine? Yeah, I heard that one, that's a great opener,' said Sean Lock.

'Yes, I'd murder for a great joke like that! How much do you want to sell it for?' laughed Jo.

'Well, you know, it's just another joke really – one of many . . .' Matt said, looking up from his set list.

'Hey, Matt, you know Eddie Odillo's a big fan of yours?' said Eddie Izzard.

'Oh yeah,' said Matt. 'We were hanging out the other night, backstage at the Apollo.'

At that point the owner of the Comedy Pit popped

his head round the door. 'Hi, Eddie, listen, no offence but I'd really like Matt to headline tonight. You OK with that, Matt?'

'I'm fine if Eddie's cool with it,' said Matt.

'Whatever's best for the show, you know,' said Eddie. 'Hey, Matt, that will make you the youngest comic to ever close the Pit!'

'Oh yeah, that's right, I'm only twelve . . .'

Matt was woken from his reverie by a high-pitched whine. He looked out of the bus window just in time to see Dave Joy on his mighty 50cc motorbike with Magda Avery on the back, her head resting on his shoulder.

'He may be cool,' thought Matt as they disappeared over the brow of the hill, 'and he may be tough and have a moustache and a motorbike and be the drummer with Toxic Cabbage, but he hasn't got a brain like mine.'

Then he reached into his blazer pocket for his little black book and scribbled 'The boy with 2 brains'.

Yes, that was an idea for a sweet little routine.

THE BOY WITH 2 BRAINS!

He was going to turn each little knock-back, every unhappy twist of Lady Luck's knife between his shoulder blades, into laughs. He'd show them all who was King of Cool.

8

Cut from a Different Cloth

As far as Matt Mills was concerned the week leading up to 'Anglebrook's Got Talent' took forever. He and Rob practised their routine every break in a disused mobile classroom (or 'The DMC' as they christened it), and most days after school at Matt's place before Ian got back from the office. They managed to persuade Ahmed to video it so they could watch it back and analyse it.

The script had developed a lot since Matt's first draft. As they'd rehearsed it, funnier ideas had occurred to him so he'd chopped and changed it around, altered the order, added in bits of business and cut bits out. He'd also found that the rhythm of the thing was important. It seemed to him you couldn't just do quick-fire gags one after the other – things needed time to breathe, to slow down occasionally and at other times speed up. He couldn't really explain how he knew this, he just kind of felt it. A bit like when he heard a piece of music and knew it was right.

With just two days to go even Ahmed was starting to get into it – chipping in ideas from behind the camera and supplying a laughter track to the video. Matt began to feel that the routine was really heading in the right direction, and as his confidence grew so did the laugh count. He wasn't concerned about the routine at all – in fact he couldn't wait to get on that assembly hall stage. No, his main concern was Rob.

Unfortunately that first wobble outside the science block hadn't been Rob's last. Oh yes, Rob had learnt the script and delivered the lines Matt had written but there was something missing. Something in his body language, the way he moved, the way he sold the gags. There was no doubt Matt was driving the thing. Rob was more interested in designing a logo for the double act than ironing out any problems within the act itself. He just didn't seem to get the same buzz out of it that Matt got.

'You gotta do something about your partner, bruv,' said Ahmed before Rob had arrived one breaktime. 'He still looks as nervous as a wasp in a fly-spray factory.'

'I know,' said Matt dolefully. 'I was hoping he would calm down as we got on top of it, but if anything, the closer the show gets the more nervous he becomes! I'm just hoping that he'll relax a bit once he hears the audience laughing.'

'IF they're laughing,' said Ahmed. 'If he don't tell them jokes right, there ain't gonna be no laughs! Jus' sayin'.'

'Thanks, Ahmed, that's really helpful,' tutted Matt. 'Now you're making *me* nervous!'

'Well, you want me to be honest, right?' said Ahmed with a shrug. 'Don't come cryin' to me when you get booed off on Friday. You gotta sort it.'

'Yeah, but how?' said Matt.

'Be honest. Tell him he's not delivering!'

'I can't,' said Matt.

'Can't what?' came a voice at the classroom door. It was Rob.

'Nothing!' said Matt.

'It's not nothin', bruv,' said Ahmed. 'We were just talking about how you don't seem so keen on doing the comedy act as Matt here.'

Rob frowned. Matt winced and looked at the floor. Ahmed was right, he needed to sort this out or it was just going to get worse.

'He's got a point, Rob. I mean, the sketch is funny and all that but I just need you to relax a bit more if we're really gonna make it work.'

'I know,' said Rob, shaking his head and leaning against a desk. 'I'm trying, Matt, but I just . . . every time I kind of get in the zone I suddenly see all these faces of people staring at me with their arms folded and they're not laughing and I get stomach cramps or wanna be sick! Actually sick!'

'Yuk!' said Ahmed, pulling a face.

'I've hardly slept a wink since you roped me into this. Every night I'm tossing and turning, worrying about forgetting my lines. Then when I do get to sleep I have this recurring nightmare where you are standing on the stage waiting for me and as I walk on to join you my trousers fall down!'

'You are one sick puppy!' said Ahmed, shaking his head.

'Every morning I wake up as normal – then I remember the gig and my stomach ties itself in knots and that sick feeling comes back.' Rob was in full flow now and seemed relieved to be getting this stuff off his chest. 'I'm thinking, where's the fun in this? Maybe I'm not cut out for show business . . .'

'It's just a lame school talent show, bruv, it ain't Vegas,' said Ahmed, but there was no stopping Rob now.

'Surely not every comedian goes through this kind of torture, or else why would anyone do it? Sometimes when we're running through it I look over at you, Matt, and I can see that look in your eye, you're lovin' it, the way you move – you're naturally funny! I always feel like I'm getting in the way of the humour, slowing it down. I'm thinking I'm just not suited to performing . . .'

He tailed off and flopped down on a chair, worn out.

Matt paused for the briefest moment, then spoke.

'Yeah, but apart from all that you're enjoying it, right?'

Rob gave out an exasperated groan and Ahmed burst out laughing.

'Nice punchline, bruv!' he said, high-fiving him.

'I hear you, Rob, I hear you,' said Matt, walking over and placing a reassuring hand on his shoulder. 'You gotta trust me, it'll be great!'

He looked over at Ahmed and held up his other hand. His first two fingers were firmly crossed.

9

The Big Day Arrives

It was the day of 'Anglebrook's Got Talent' and in number 77 Bathurst Street Matt Mills's alarm clock rang out, but in Matt's bed there was no movement at all. He'd already been up for half an hour. He hadn't been able to sleep that night either, but unlike Rob his insomnia was due to excitement! He couldn't wait for the big day to dawn. He'd bounded out of bed, slapped a wet flannel round his face, checked his nose for bogeys and headed down to the kitchen to cook himself a fry-up.

'Someone's in a good mood,' said Ian, dipping a piece of toast into the yolk of Matt's fried egg.

'Yeah, well, it's the school talent show,' said Matt, shifting his plate so that Ian couldn't get to it. 'Me and Rob's first gig as Mills and Brown.'

'Don't get your hopes up,' said Ian. 'Prepare to have your dreams shattered. Hardest job in the world, comedy, so they say, and there hasn't been a funny double act since, well, since Morecambe and Wise.'

'Who?' said Matt.

'Morecambe and Wise – you know,' and with that Ian sprang to his feet and started to do a weird dance, kicking his legs up in turn and putting alternate hands behind his head as he did so.

'I think maybe you need a holiday, Ian,' said Matt.

MORECAMBE AND WISE

Double act from the North of England. Massive in the 1970s. Eric Morecambe – funny man, Ernie Wise – straight man.

Examples:
'I'm playing all the right notes
but not necessarily in the
right order!'

'He's got short fat hairy legs!'

'Huh!' said Ian, sitting back down and buttering another piece of toast. 'I was like you once, full of ideas for the future. Big plans, ambitions . . . all gone up in smoke.'

'When was this exactly?' said Matt. 'World War Two?'

Ian let out a big sigh. 'All right, Captain Sarcastic!' he said, snatching a piece of bacon off Matt's plate and heading for the door.

'Thanks for wishing me luck!' Matt called after him. 'Adults, they're just trouble,' he thought. Then he reached excitedly into his pocket for his little black book and wrote: 'Kids looking after adults as if they were the kids.' Yes, he could see the idea of turning the tables on the child-adult relationship might be a nice little routine.

KIDS LOOKING AFTER ADULTS - IDEAS

Stop your dad from drinking beer by saying he can't watch Match of the Day.

Telling Mum not to wear so much make-up.

Changing wi-fi code so you can watch your stuff and they can't.

Make their packed lunch for them- see how they like dry sandwiches every day.

Bedtime - 'No you can't stay up! You've got work tomorrow!'

Take their phones away from them
so they can't text their friends
or do Facebook/Twitter.

Choose their clothes for them.

Decide what they eat — ban
fancy food, more chips!!

There was the 'Ping!' of a message arriving on his phone. He peered over at it. It was from Rob.

'I'm ill. Not going in today. You'll have to do the show without me. Rob.'

'What?!'

Matt snatched the phone off the table and pressed Call. He stood up and started pacing up and down. His mind was in turmoil, blind panic.

'Hello?' said a weak voice on the other end.

Matt jumped straight in.

'You can't do this, Rob! You agreed! We've been rehearsing all week!'

'It's just not me, Matt! You're much better on your own.'

'No, no way! The day of the gig? You can't do this to me!' said Matt, thrusting his free hand angrily into the air. 'I'll be there with you. It's just . . . it's just first-night nerves, that's all.'

'But . . .'

'No buts! Talk to the hand!' he said, holding his hand up flat to the phone.

'What hand?' came Rob's weak voice in reply. 'I can't see a hand.'

'That's cos it's a phone, you . . . dork!' said Matt. He was almost shouting now. 'I'm holding my hand, flat, up in your face! Now I don't want to hear any more about it. The show must go on, remember?'

'I've been sick!' replied Rob, his voice catching as if he was close to tears.

Matt realised immediately that anger wasn't going

to help the situation. He took a deep breath and tried to calm down.

'You can do it, I know you can,' he said, faking a calm voice as best he could. 'You're just a little out of your comfort zone.'

'I'm so far out of it I can't even remember what it looks like!' groaned Rob.

'Look, come into school and let's talk about it face to face. If you're still not happy then, well, I'll come up with another plan.'

'Well, I'm not sure . . .' stuttered Rob. 'My mum said I should really stay home today.'

'Let me talk to her.'

'Eh?'

'Let me talk to your mum. Put her on the line.'

'Er, OK . . . hang on . . .'

Matt could hear Rob calling out to his mum, then his little sister Trish taking up the call and repeating it. Then came the click-clack of heels on a kitchen floor and the wailing of Rob's baby brother – getting louder as she got closer.

'Hello? Who's this?' said Rob's mum, sounding a bit frazzled.

'Er, it's ... it's ... Meredith Pavey, Mrs Brown!' said Matt, lowering his voice abruptly.

'Oh!' said Rob's mum. 'Mr Pavey! How can I help?'

'I sincerely hope you can help, Mrs Brown!' said Matt as a plan started to hatch in his head. 'I'm phoning all the parents this morning—'

'What? All six hundred of them?'

'Er ... yes! I'm calling them all, in alphabetical order, about a mysterious sickness that's affecting some of our pupils.'

'Oh yes?' said Mrs Brown. 'Our Robert said he was feeling sick.'

'Ah! Then it's just as well I called. You see, it's a new virus ...'

'Oh!'

'Yes, called ... um ... RAW Virus ... It's come over from, um ... the Isle of Wight ... Nothing to be worried about – that is, provided young

Robert gets the antidote within forty-five minutes.'

'Forty-five minutes? But that's no time at all! What happens if he doesn't get it?' said Rob's mum, clearly anxious, the baby now screaming at the top of his voice.

'Um, well . . . in extreme cases his nose will turn blue and drop off and possibly his willy too!'

'What was that?' said Rob's mum.

'There's no time for chit-chat, Mrs B,' said Matt. 'We must act fast! Fortunately we have a limited supply of the antidote, which Matron is giving out on a first-come, first-served basis. So if you could bring young Robert in as quickly as . . . hello?'

The line had gone dead. Mrs Brown and 'young Robert' had already left the the house.

Within five minutes of Matt arriving at the school gates he heard a squeal of tyres and looked up to see Mrs Brown, Rob and Trish getting out of the family hatchback. She trotted up to the gates pushing Rob in front of her with one arm, the still-screaming baby in the other. Matt could tell she was at the end of her tether. 'You here for the RAW Virus antidote?' he said, stepping forward to meet them.

'I don't wanna catch it!' wailed Trish as she ran past him and into the playground.

'Yes! Where do we go?' snapped Rob's mum.

'Mr Pavey told me to take him straight through to Matron,' said Matt.

'He's not going anywhere without me!' said Rob's mum.

'I'm afraid that won't be possible, Mrs Brown,' said Matt. 'Due to quarantine, and, uh, the baby. So you'd better get back in your car before you catch it too!'

Mrs Brown hesitated for a moment. She was about to give Rob a goodbye kiss, but thought better of it. She turned, trotted back to her car, strapped the baby in and sped off as fast as she'd arrived.

'RAW Virus?' said Rob dubiously.

'Rob's A Wimp!' said Matt with a grin. 'I knew you wouldn't back out!'

RAW

(ROB'S A WIMP VIRUS)

'I didn't have much choice, did I? I'd rather die on stage than have my willy drop off!'

RAW (Rob's A Wimp) Virus

Symptoms
· Nausea
· Insomnia
· Starting to think you're not funny
· Inclined to let down close friends
· Backing out of important engagements

Signs
· Nose turns blue and drops off
· Willy gets smaller then drops off
· Generally look a bit of a wimp

Treatment
Stop complaining and get on with it!

Matt laughed and shook Rob's hand. 'You've got your outfit, right?' he asked excitedly.

'Yeah, I think so,' said Rob.

'You think so?!' said Matt hopping up and down like a duck on a biscuit tin that's got a candle burning inside it.

'OK, yes, I've got the outfit!' said Rob.

'Good. We'll meet at first break in Greggs to have a sausage roll and run the lines.'

'Can you not talk about food please,' groaned Rob, rubbing his stomach and pulling a pained expression. 'It's just that I'm still feeling queasy.'

'OK,' said Matt. 'Let's meet by the science block instead. Relax. It's gonna be great.'

'I wish everyone would stop telling me to relax!' said Rob, shaking his head as he walked off to his first lesson.

Matt had never known a morning take so long. Double maths felt like about two hundred years. Every time he looked up at the clock the hands had hardly moved at all. First break came and went, he met up with Rob and they ran the routine – or at least tried to. Rob kept fluffing his lines. He assured Matt that he knew them, that it was just nerves, but it didn't bode well. Lunch break was the same. If anything, Rob was even flakier – a couple of times he just froze. Three or four times he'd tried to back out again. With a mixture of firm handling and gentle persuasion Matt managed to keep him on course for the show and in fact their last run-through hadn't gone badly at all.

Finally the bell rang for the start of afternoon school and all the kids piled into the assembly hall. The moment of Mills and Brown's debut had arrived.

10

Fame Stands Tiptoe in the Wings

'Hello? Testing, one-two, one-two . . . ? Is this on?'
said Mr Gillingham, fumbling around with the
microphone. He wore a red-squinned jacket and had
taken the stage in the assembly hall in front of pretty
much the entire school, from year sixes all the way up
to sixth formers, to just a ripple of applause.

'WWWwwwwwwaaaaang!' A great big howl of
feedback rang out.

'Ah, that seems to be working,' he muttered.
'Ahem. Ladies and gentlemen, welcome to the very
first "Anglebrook's Got Talent!"'

It was then that the crowd went wild, clapping,

cheering and stamping their feet – one year six boy even threw his shoes in the air. It sounded to Matt like a herd of wildebeest charging through the hall, ridden by chimpanzees.

CHIMPANZEES
RIDING
WILDEBEEST!

'This is gonna be epic,' he whispered to his sidekick as they stood backstage, watching proceedings through a chink in the curtains.

To Rob that sound was one of the most frightening noises he'd ever heard in his life. 'I need to go to the loo!' he groaned, and dashed off towards the exit.

Out front, Mr Gillingham was introducing the judges – Mrs McGregor the drama teacher, Mr Avery the PE teacher (and Magda's dad), and an elderly gent by the name of Thomas Finlayson, who had apparently once been an actor in the West End and lived in the town.

Up first was a year six boy, Neil Trottman – ten years old with a big afro and about as tall as a French loaf.

'He looks about two!' said Matt, peeking through the curtains.

'What on earth is he wearing?' whispered Rob, back from his visit to the toilet block with his breath smelling of sick. It was a good point. Little Neil had on brown sandals with white knee-length socks leading to a pair of blue cotton shorts, a short-sleeved Fred Perry shirt, a striped tank top and a spotted bow tie. The whole rig-out was topped with a straw boater secured with a strip of elastic that went under his chin.

'He's going to get crucified in that lot!' agreed Matt.

'Ladies and gentlemen, put your hands together for Neil Trottman!' Mr Gillingham announced with a flourish and on Neil jogged.

'Go, girlfriend!' said Matt and they both laughed.

There was a wolf whistle from somewhere at the back of the hall and Matt could see Mr G heading off to where it had come from to prevent it from happening again.

Neil stood centre stage with his back to the audience. He turned and gave a signal to Ahmed in the wings, who had managed to wangle himself the job of operating the sound. Ahmed pressed Play on the CD player and the opening chords of CeeLo Green's 'Forget You' filled the hall. Suddenly little Neil Trottman came alive, kicking his legs up, jack-knifing his body, moonwalking, body-popping – the lot.

'Blimey!' said Matt, turning to Rob open-mouthed. 'What did HE have for breakfast?!'

As he watched Neil, for the first time since they'd entered the talent show Matt felt nervous. It dawned on him that this was a competition and as such there were bound to be some other really talented people competing against them.

He heard a gasp and looked back out at Master

Trottman's display: the little lad had dropped to the floor and was now spinning round and round on his back. The crowd were loving every minute of it, clapping along and stamping their feet. Some of the sixth-form girls had started a Mexican wave. As the song came to an end Neil jumped into the air and landed in the splits, to a cheer from the girls and a wince from the boys. The audience were suddenly on their feet, cheering and applauding.

'Neil Trottman, ladies and gentlemen!' bellowed Mr Gillingham with a big smile. 'What a way to start the show! Big things come in small packages indeed!'

'Wow, that was awesome! Well done!' said Matt, slapping Neil on the back as he walked past them.

'Thanks, man, it's my mum really! She was a dancer for a while back in Jamaica, so I guess it's in my genes,' he panted, trying to catch his breath. 'The outfit was her idea too. She said it would lower people's expectations, so that when I actually turned out to be not that bad it would have double the impact.'

'Well, she was right!' said Matt.

'When are you up?' asked Neil, taking off his bow tie and stuffing it into his boater.

'After this next lot.'

'Well, good luck, they seem like a nice crowd.'

'Who's ready to rock?!' called Mr Gillingham. He was really starting to enjoy his role of MC. 'Let me hear you make some noise for Toxic Cabbage!'

Matt, Rob and Neil were almost knocked over as Dave Joy and his band of merry men pushed past them, reeking of hair gel and sweat, and took up their positions.

Matt and Rob peeked out at them from the wings. They certainly looked the part – decked out in leather jackets and matching 'Toxic Cabbage' T-shirts, and with their hair spiked up with gel – but then it's hard not to look cool with a drum kit between your legs or an electric guitar slung round your neck.

'Why Toxic Cabbage?' said Matt to no one in particular.

'They meant to call themselves Toxic Garbage, but the bloke who printed the T-shirts misread it,' said Ahmed, deftly pushing up one of the faders on his mixing desk. 'They like it nice and loud.'

'Thraaaaaaaang!' There was an ear-splitting howl of electric guitar that wasn't quite a chord.

'Good evening Anglebrook! I'm Freddie Metcalfe and we are Toxic Cabbage!' yelled the lead singer.

'One, two, three, four!' shouted Dave from behind his drum kit and he started smashing the heck out of it. The guitarist and bass player attacked their instruments in similar style and Freddie didn't so much sing as spit out the self-penned lyrics to their song.

'Maths is boring! School's for morons! Maths is boring! School's for morons!' he screamed. 'Society's a failure, do yourself a favour, just turn on the telly and chiiiiiiiiiiiiill!'

'Hmm,' whispered Matt. 'It's hardly Shakespeare, is it, Rob?'

But Rob didn't reply.

'Rob?' Matt looked round but it wasn't Rob standing next to him, it was Ahmed.

'Sick, aren't they, bruv?' said Ahmed, brimming with admiration. 'They're dead right, what's the point of school . . . ?'

But Matt wasn't listening. 'You seen Rob?'

'He went that way a couple of minutes ago,' said Ahmed, pointing to the exit.

'Rob?' called Matt, a feeling of panic bubbling up

in his chest. 'Where are you?' he muttered as he strode down the steps and through the corridor towards the changing rooms. But Rob was nowhere to be seen.

'Rob?!' he called. He was running now – they only had a few minutes before they were on.

'You seen Rob Brown?' he asked a year five girl dressed as a chicken.

'No. Oi, mind my wings! They're only crepe paper!'

'Rob?!' Matt called out, leaning into the boys' changing rooms. 'Anyone seen him?' All he got back was a lot of blank faces.

Matt's mind was churning. 'He wouldn't have run out on me, would he?' He knew Rob was nervous about the show but surely he wouldn't have just cut and run?

He dashed into the loos and there leaning over the sink was the crumpled, pasty-faced figure of Rob Brown.

'Rob?!! What . . . ?'

'I've been sick again,' moaned Rob, holding a hanky up to his mouth.

'You'd better check your willy hasn't dropped off

too,' said Matt lamely, trying to cheer his mate up.

'Oh don't, Matt, please. I'm a bag of nerves! I can't go on like this!'

'Listen!' said Matt firmly, trying his best to keep a lid on his own growing feeling of panic. 'It's no problem, have a glass of water, take a couple of deep breaths. Here, have one of these to take away the taste.' He reached into his pocket and offered Rob a mint.

Before Rob had a chance to answer, Ahmed appeared at the end of the corridor and screamed at them. 'Oy! You two! Mills and Brown! You're on!'

'Ooooh!' groaned Rob.

'Come on!' cried Matt. 'We've got no choice now!' He grabbed Rob's arm and dragged him down the corridor towards the assembly hall.

Back on stage, Toxic Cabbage had finished to stunned silence. 'Rock 'n' roll!' screamed Dave Joy, kicking over the microphone stand as he marched off.

'Well, somebody's very angry!' joked Mr Gillingham, picking up the microphone from the floor and wiping the spit off it with his hanky.

'Right, hopefully our next act is a bit more cheerful . . .'

'Eughgh!' groaned Rob, coughing up the last few bits of sick into his mouth and peering across at the stage. 'What are they?'

'What are what?' said Matt, his eyes firmly fixed on the audience.

'Those poles, what are they for?'

'They're microphone stands, you derr-brain!' snapped Matt. This really was the limit.

'But we've never practised with microphones!' said Rob, his voice shaking with fear.

'Oh for the love of fudge!' moaned Matt. 'You do the same act, it's just that you speak your words into the microphone!'

'How do you . . .'

But there wasn't time for Rob to complete his sentence. Mr Gillingham was already halfway through their introduction.

'Ladies and gentlemen, you've all read their jokes in "Pavey's Punchlines", now's your chance to meet them in the flesh. From the guys that brought you School Dinner Bingo – put your hands together for the comic stylings of Mills and Brown!'

'Dead men walking!' sang Ahmed, pushing up the fader on their intro music. 'Microphones now live!'

There was a surprisingly good response to their intro. Matt bounded on and got to the mic first with Rob walking sheepishly behind him. If you could read body language, his was screaming 'I don't want to be here'. It reminded Matt of the old gag about the ugly child: 'My parents made me walk into a room backwards so that people would think I was leaving.'

GAGS ABOUT APPEARANCE
Kid: 'The other kids say I look like a monkey.'
Mother: 'Take no notice. Now go upstairs and comb your face!'

Man: 'I took my wife to see
Frankenstein.'
Friend: 'There must have been a
lot of screaming.'
Man: 'I thought he'd never stop!'

She looked like a character
witness for a nightmare!

He looked like a million dollars—all
green and crumpled!

He looked like the first husband
of a widow!

She was so ugly she could model
for death threats.

The audience sat forward in anticipation as Matt picked up the microphone.

'Go, Rob!' came a little girl's voice from somewhere in the middle of the throng – it was Rob's sister, Trish.

'Afternoon! We've got a little cookery lesson for you,' said Matt. There was a titter from the front row, then a laugh as Rob dislodged the microphone from the stand and sent it crashing to the floor.

'Ha ha!' Matt laughed nervously. 'Butterfingers!'

He could hear two voices now, one coming from his mouth, the other inside his head offering him a running commentary: *What did you say that for? You need to do something to get a laugh – and quick.*

What Matt hadn't been ready for was how little he could see of the audience. The spotlight was so bright that all he could make out were rough outlines and silhouettes and a few faces in the front row, which were a ghostly silver from the light reflected off the stage.

'Hey, Rob, what's the menu for today?' said Matt. He could feel his mouth getting dry, like he'd been crawling through the Gobi Desert whilst chewing on a packet of Jacob's cream crackers. His lips were starting to stick to his teeth and his tongue to the roof of his mouth. Matt waited a beat for Rob to speak, but heard nothing. Matt looked over. Rob's face was still white, only now it had a sheen of sweat over it. His mouth was opening and closing but no sound was coming out. He looked like a fish out of water, a beached shark gasping for breath on the deck of a Japanese fishing trawler, which in many ways he was. Matt recognised it straight away – Rob was frozen.

Unfortunately it wasn't just Rob who was having a problem remembering his lines now. The backstage drama prior to coming on had rattled Matt too. What he'd really needed was a few moments of calm to run the lines with Rob and collect his thoughts, not the other half of the double act throwing up and trying to back out of it.

At this point you could have cut the air into slices with a knife, fried them in a pan and served them with baked beans. Matt looked at the few faces he could see in the crowd. All of them were wide-eyed with expectancy, hoping to be entertained.

Then something kicked in. Call it a survival instinct, call it chutzpah, call it destiny, maybe it was a showbiz god somewhere taking his hand and leading him through, or maybe it was the very thing that he was being tested for – talent – but suddenly Matt had an idea.

'Do you do any other fish impressions, Rob?' he said. There was a smattering of laughter that Matt knew instinctively he had to capitalise on.

'Hey, I bumped into Mr Pavey outside. I hear they've come up with a new cure for baldness,' said Matt, stepping forward and fixing his eyes on the back of the room. 'It doesn't actually grow hair, it just shrinks your head to make the most of the hair you've got!'

The smattering turned into a big laugh. 'Yeah, Pavey's got this stuff at home, you put it on your head and it gives you a full head of hair with enough for a pony tail down the back – it's a squirrel!'

The big laugh turned into a wave of laughter.

'And those glasses! As soon as he put them on the insults started – Four-eyes! Gogglebox! Speccy! – Well, Pavey wasn't having that. He said, "I don't have to listen to this – you're not the only optician in Anglebrook!"'

The wave turned into a roar. Matt looked round at Rob, who seemed slightly less anxious. He nodded to him. Rob nodded back.

'Right!' shouted Matt. 'We're here to show you how to cook your sister's Harry Styles doll!' With that they both reached into their coats and whipped out their dolls. Another huge wave of laughter and a big cheer too from some of the blokes at the back of the hall. Matt caught Rob's eye and winked. They were off!

The next five minutes were some of the best of Matt Mills's short life so far. The laughs came thick and fast and where jokes fell flat he was able to step in with an ad lib and bring it back round. It was like riding a bucking bronco – exciting, exhilarating, dangerous, never sure if he was going to get thrown off or tame it and ride it home. Even Rob looked like he was enjoying himself. In fact sometimes he was laughing at Matt's ad libs as much as the audience.

'It does tend to swell up a bit!' said Matt and Rob together, producing a cooked roast chicken from a carrier bag. Then came the killer punchline.

'. . . But so would you if you had no bum hole!'

The kids in the hall were beside themselves. The year sixes couldn't believe their ears and were rocking back in their seats, the sixth formers were nodding approvingly, looking at each other, cheering and whistling.

'We are Mills and Brown!' shouted Matt over the din. 'That's all from us . . . Good—'

Then nothing.

Matt finished the sign-off so favoured by stand-ups the world over but no sound came out of the speakers. Matt tapped the microphone like he'd seen them do on TV, then looked across at Ahmed in the wings. Leaning over him was Mr Pavey. As he straightened up Matt could see he was holding something in his hand. It was the other end of the microphone lead. If looks could kill, Matt and Rob would have been dead, cremated and buried at sea.

'Ooops! Looks like the game's up!' said Rob. 'What do we do now?'

'Keep playing for laughs,' hissed Matt through a fixed grin. Mr P was now striding across the stage straight towards them, his face looking like a screwed-up crisp packet.

'That's enough of that rubbish!' he snarled at Mills and Brown.

There was a lone 'Boo!' from one of the braver sixth formers.

'I'll see you in my office after school!' snapped Pavey. The vein on his head now resembled the aerial view of the River Thames as seen on the opening titles of *Eastenders*. 'There's more blood in his head than the whole of the rest of his body,' thought Matt. 'If that pops he'll die!'

Rob was back to his pre-show, ashen-faced, nervous look.

Matt peered across at Ahmed, who gave him the thumbs up. Matt tapped the mic and sure enough it was live again. 'We'd like to thank our special guest, Mr Pavey! That's all from us – goodnight!' he cracked, handing the mic to Mr P. Well, that just about lifted the roof. Matt and Rob hightailed it into the wings, leaving Pavey stranded in the spotlight.

'That was baaaaad!' howled Ahmed, slapping them both on the back. 'Nice knowing you, guys! You are gonna get murdered.' Pretty soon they were surrounded by kids congratulating them, patting them, high-fiving them, shaking their hands and generally bigging them up with cries of 'Awesome!', 'Dope!' and 'Sick!'

Matt and Rob felt about ten feet tall.

The crowd suddenly parted and there she was – Magda Avery. The light from the stage behind her gave her something approaching a halo. 'You were soooooo funny!' she giggled. 'But you are gonna be in such trouble.'

'Thanks, we do it for Anglebrook!' said Matt, punching the air. 'We're not so much comedians as freedom fighters! The all-conquering power of comedy!'

'Yeah,' said Magda, her face suddenly grey.

'You OK?' asked Matt. 'When are you on?'

'I'm on next. Bit nervy to be honest.'

'Don't worry, you'll be fine,' said Matt. 'You look just like her.'

It was true: her mum had styled the wig into Adele's big trademark hair and somehow Magda had managed to transform her face into that of the multi-million-record-selling songbird.

'Yeah, I'm pleased with how it's turned out. It's what I want to do really. Not just fashion make-up but special effects for films.'

'Oh man, that would be so cool!' said Rob. 'Like when they age people up to look a hundred or something?'

'Yeah,' said Magda. 'Or like when they make someone look really fat or . . .'

'You're on, Magda!' interrupted Ahmed.

'Ooops! Excuse me! Wish me luck!' she said, turning towards the stage.

'Good luck!' said Matt, Rob and Ahmed in unison.

She looked great as she walked towards the microphone. Like a real star.

'She's the one to beat,' thought Matt.

Then Magda opened her mouth and started to sing.

They were musical notes, certainly, just not the right ones for the tune she was supposed to be singing. She sounded like a cat being strangled by its own ball of string.

'Good grief,' said Matt, turning to Rob. 'She sounds flatter than a pancake in a trouser press! It's like asthma set to music! Like a cow that's just trodden on its own udder!'

She finished to a few claps that never quite became a round of applause and crossed to the wings.

'How'd it look?' she asked, appearing a little crestfallen.

'It *looked* fine,' said Matt. He could see she was upset.

'Hey! Don't worry about it, you did your best, that's all you can do!' said Rob, stepping forward to put a comforting hand on her shoulder.

'Oh God, it was a disaster!' she said. Her eyes filled with tears, her shoulders started to heave and out came a full-blown sob, tears streaming down her face and snot starting to bubble out of her nose. There was nothing for it. Rob put his arms round her and gave her a hug, and – miracle of miracles – she hugged him back. In fact she held on to him like a limpet as she let all the stress and humiliation of her very public failure flood out – all over Rob's shirt.

'Oi!' came a loud voice.

Rob turned round just in time to see Dave Joy swinging his fist at his face.

'Nnnnnrghhhh!'

Rob ducked, just as Ahmed was walking past with a mic stand. WHUMP! went the fist straight into Ahmed's nose. Ahmed let out a cry of pain like a wounded animal, went cross-eyed, tottered backwards, then fell into Matt's arms.

'Aaaaaaaaaaaaaaaaaaagh!' Magda Avery screamed at the top of her voice.

'That's the best note you've hit all day!' quipped Matt. Then he saw Dave advancing towards him.

'Rob! run for it!' he cried. And with that they hoofed it down the stairs from the wings and along the corridor, bashing into various contestants and bits of scenery as they went.

'RRRRrraaaaar!' screamed Dave Joy as he tripped over the year five in the chicken costume, sending her sprawling to the floor. 'Come 'ere, you!'

Matt and Rob burst through the swing doors from the main hall, out into the cool air of the playground, and cast around for somewhere to hide.

'Where to now?' panted Rob, holding his side to combat his rapidly developing stitch.

'Greggs?' suggested Rob.

'That's the first place he'll try!' said Matt, equally out of breath. They could hear the Neanderthal thump of Dave's feet coming down the corridor behind them.

'What's the one place he would never venture into?'

They both looked at each other and laughed: 'The library!' And they ran off across the playground to the main block.

11

A Change in Line-up

'Listen, Matt, I'm sorry,' said Rob as they sought sanctuary between the bookcases of the fusty, wood-panelled library. With pretty much the entire school at the talent show it was deserted.

'It wasn't your fault. I shouldn't have pushed you into it. I'd hoped you were as keen as me,' said Matt, climbing up on a chair and looking through one of the high windows, scouring the playground for any sight of Dave Joy. 'By the way, you'll have to explain to your mum why you've got Adele's make-up all over your shirt.'

Rob took out his phone and used the camera to

study Magda's make-up stains all over his shoulder. 'Anyway, I'm resigning,' he said.

'Resigning?'

'Yeah. I want out of the double act, and this time I mean it.'

'Oh come on, Rob, stick with it, I'm begging you!' said Matt, climbing down off the chair and dropping to one knee.

'You can do it better on your own, Matt! You know I'm just slowing you down.'

'But what will we tell the fans?!' pleaded Matt.

'You can't be serious for a *moment*, can you?' Rob said, feeling rather foolish.

'We're getting an urgent news flash through from Anglebrook!' said Matt, affecting a newsreader-style voice. 'Apparently hundreds of Mills and Brown fans are devastated at the news that the hit double act, who only ever did half a gig, in a school, to a bunch of losers, are due to split. We go live to our reporter at the scene . . .'

Rob started laughing. 'Well, if you put it like that I might stay.'

'Then I resign!' said Matt. 'Look on the bright side, Rob, at least we weren't as bad as Magda.'

'Is that right?' came a voice from behind them.

'How do you do that?' asked Matt, running a hand through his thick mop of hair. It was Magda.

'Do what?' she said.

'Creep up on me just as I'm making a fool of myself? Anyway, when I said it was bad I meant in the Michael Jackson sense of the word – where bad means good. Oh man, dat was BAAAAD!' Matt span round and moonwalked backwards, tripped over a chair and landed on his bottom on the floor.

'You are somethin' else, Matt Mills!' said Magda, reaching down to help him back up. 'You didn't mean it that way, but you were right, I can't sing for toffee. I don't know what I was thinking. It was Dave's idea, he egged me on.' She brightened up. 'You two did all right though! You would have won if you hadn't been disqualified.'

'Disqualified?!' said Matt in disbelief.

'Yeah, they said it was inappropriate. So that squirt Neil Trottman won. Mind you, he was pretty nifty on his feet. Like I said though, you were dead funny.'

'Yeah?' said Matt, a proud grin breaking out on his face. 'Hear that, Rob? We've got a fan.'

'Not Rob so much as you,' she said. 'Him standing staring at you, I couldn't work out if that was part of the act or he'd just forgotten his lines. No, I think he's got other strengths.'

'Sadly, Ms Avery, you are not the only one. Mr Brown here is thinking of resigning from show business – the shortest career on the stage since the lead flea in the flea circus caught fire jumping over his trainer's birthday cake.'

'There you go again, always making jokes about everything.'

'That's what I just said!' said Rob.

But Matt wasn't listening. He'd taken out his little black book and was scribbling in it.

STUNT FLEA ROUTINE
(SHAGGY DOG STORY!!.)

Flea lives on Pavey's head but
starving (no hair!)
• Rides into town on a dog
• Joins flea circus
• Trainer trains him to jump
over stuff
• Decides to surprise him for his
birthday – Jumps over cake
• Catches fire (Tiny wheelchair?) –
retires to teach (!!!) (Better
punchline??.)

'Where's Dave, anyway?' Rob asked Magda.

'I sent him off with a flea in his ear,' said Magda
with a wry smile.

'Did you get his address?' asked Matt, raising his
pen above his notebook in readiness.

'Dave's? I already know it!'

'Not Dave's, the *flea's* – it's just that the circus are looking for a lead stunt flea.'

'Get outta here!' laughed Magda, whacking Matt playfully with her bag. 'Anyway, I sorted out Dave. I explained Rob was just being nice.'

'She's great isn't she?' said Rob wistfully as they watched Magda across the playground from the library window.

'I think I'm slowly breaking her down,' said Matt.

'In your dreams,' said Rob with a sigh. 'I still feel really bad about the talent show.'

'Well don't. That's showbiz. The important thing is we learnt something.'

'Yeah – that I'm no cop at it,' said Rob.

'Hmm. There is one way you can be involved in my career as a stand-up comic, Rob.'

'Yeah?'

'Yeah. I'll need a manager.'

'A manager?'

'Yup. To book gigs, give advice and generally help guide my upwards trajectory to the stars.'

'What's the pay like?' shot back Rob. 'I'll want fifteen per cent of gross earnings.'

'What's fifteen per cent of nothing?' said Matt.

'I'm in!' said Rob.

'Together but apart!' said Matt. 'Now we've got a meeting with destiny.' He put his arm round his ex-comedy partner's shoulders and headed for the door, the sound of the audience's laughter still ringing in his ears.

12

Ng Ning Ning!

As they left the library and headed towards Mr Pavey's office the last stragglers were filing out of 'Anglebrook's Got Talent'.

'Dis is all your fault,' said Ahmed, walking up to them and pointing to his nose, which was now sporting a large bandage. He sounded, well, he sounded like his nose was sporting a very large bandage. 'Nuckily ith not moken.'

'What'd he say?' said Rob.

'Nuckily ith not moken,' said Matt with a grin. 'It's rhyming slang for "Luckily it's not broken".

I hear Trottman won?'

'Yeah, I nean he looked like a right mratt but dat dancing. I never knew he had it in him.'

'Yes, he's a dark horse all right.'

'Shame about Mills and Brown – especially the Brown bit.'

'All right wise guy, stow it or I'll make the rest of your face match that nose,' said Rob, putting on an American gangster voice. He was much more his old self now he'd stepped out of the shadow of the talent show.

'Pavey's face was priceless when you were doing all that stuff about him being bald,' laughed Ahmed.

'Yeah, and shortly we're going to be paying for it,' said Matt. 'We're due in his office in ten minutes and I'm pretty sure it won't be to offer us the post of joint head boy.'

Ahmed snorted out a laugh. 'Oww!' he whined. 'It hurts my doze every time I laugh.'

'Listen, Ahmed, I'm really sorry about your doze – I mean nose. What can I say – Dave overreacted,' said Rob.

'Who'd a fort, you and Nagda Abery!'

'Hey! There's nothing going on between Rob and Nagda – I mean Magda . . .' interjected Matt.

'Chance'd be a fine thing,' chipped in Rob.

'He was merely comforting her on the demise of her singing career, m'lud,' said Matt, as if Rob was the accused in a trial. 'Call the first witness!' he said, warming to the courtroom theme. 'Dave Joy!'

Matt bent himself over slightly, stuck out his chin, pressed his nose flat against his face with his finger and swung his other arm about like a caveman. 'Nnnngnng! Nag! Ning!' he grunted.

'I put it to you, Mr Joy, that you did wilfully punch one Ahmed Chalabi in the nose, causing him to sound like an advert for decongestant nasal spray!' laughed Rob, with one hand on the lapel of his jacket like a barrister. 'How do you plead?'

'Ng ning ning!' yelled Matt, jumping up and down and waving his hands around in the air above his head.

'Ng ning ning?' said Rob, looking surprised.

'Ng ning ning!' repeated Matt, making sounds like a chimp and lying on his back, kicking both arms and legs in the air.

'Not guilty, m'lud!' said Rob, trying hard not to laugh.

'You two are a couple of nutters,' said Ahmed, turning to leave and bumping into the hulking great figure of Dave Joy himself.

'Aargh!' squealed Ahmed, jumping a good six inches off the floor. 'Please don't hit me! . . . Again!' he said, putting his hands up to his face defensively. He then felt two hands clamp on to his arms – but it wasn't Dave, it was Rob.

'I can explain!' cried Rob, crouching behind his hapless friend.

'He was merely comforting Magda at the demise of her singing career!' sang Matt, trying to help his friends out.

'I know,' said Dave, looking uncharacteristically contrite. 'She told me. Anyway, she's got better taste than to hang out with a mug like you.'

'He accepts your apology!' said Matt. Rob let go of Ahmed and took a pace back out of Dave's considerable reach just in case he changed his mind.

'Bless! He gets very possessive,' said Magda, joining the throng and putting her arm around Dave's waist. 'I explained we just had a cuddle because I was upset over the singing thing.'

'Exactly. Rob was merely doing what any one of us would have done in the circumstances.'

'Watch it, you!' said Dave, narrowing his eyes at Matt.

Magda gave him a dig in the ribs with her elbow.

'Ahem. I'm sorry, Ahmed,' said Dave, remembering why he'd been dragged there. 'You got caught in the middle. How's your nose?'

'Twice as big as it should be, thanks,' said Ahmed, 'but nothing's broken.'

'You live in Staplefirst, don't you?' said Dave. 'I'll give you a lift home on the bike if you like.'

'Um, it was bad enough nearly breaking my nose, never mind my neck,' said Ahmed. 'I'll give that a miss, thanks, Dave.'

'Well, I owe you one,' said Dave, offering his hand to Ahmed, who shook it weakly.

'Come on then, Dave, you've done your sorrys!' chirped Magda, turning to leave. As she did, Dave leant over to Matt and whispered in his ear. 'Watch your step, Mills, you may be funny but next time you won't be laughing. I'm watching you – and your mate.'

Matt and Rob both swallowed hard.

'Coming, sweetheart!' called Dave cheerily to Magda, fixing first Matt then Rob with his death stare. Then he stomped off after her.

'Phew! That was a close one,' said Matt, straightening his glasses and running a hand through his hair. 'If he'd turned up a few moments earlier . . .'

'You'd have been mincemeat,' said Rob.

'Pooh! His breath stank too. I'd recognise that smell anywhere,' said Matt, screwing up his face.

'Yeah? What did it smell of?'

'Toxic Cabbage!' said Matt and all three of them started laughing.

13

A Hair-raising Encounter with the Head

'When Mrs McGregor came to me with the idea of a school talent show I had my doubts!' barked Mr Pavey, leaning over his desk and glaring at Matt and Rob, who were seated on the other side. 'I felt that this sort of popular entertainment had no place in an establishment of learning. Do the lower years, for instance, really need to be exposed to Toxic Cabbage and a dancing Trottman when we have the works of Beethoven, Mozart and Shakespeare? However, Mrs McGregor was passionate about the project, she is an extremely ... ahem ... forthright ... member of my staff. She made the case that it is important for young people to experience all sides of our culture from the soaring heights of, well, Beethoven, as I have already detailed, to the considerable lows of a boy dancing in a bow tie and straw boater. So, not to dampen her ... enthusiasm ... I agreed to let the show go ahead and for a few moments I was carried along with the general excitement of the occasion. I had to agree that in the early stages it had a certain innocent fun. That innocence was completely blackened the moment you stepped on to the stage! You took it into your heads to hijack what up until that moment had been a reasonably entertaining, if rather primitive, display of talent and turn it into a tawdry and insulting diatribe about the matter of my unfortunate hair loss and ... well ... general appearance.'

At the mention of Mr Pavey's baldness Matt could feel a laugh bubbling up inside him, struggling to get out.

Pavey fixed Matt with a withering look and leant in to within an inch of his face. Matt could smell a mixture of egg and toast on his breath, mixed with the tang of instant coffee. Mr P paused for a moment, then continued: 'And don't even think about laughing!' he shouted, showering Matt's glasses with tiny specks of egg, toast and coffee-stained saliva.

He straightened himself up, turned and walked over to the glass-fronted bookcase. As he peered at his dim reflection his hand wandered up to touch the hairless dome that crowned his head. His voice dropped into a lower register and he spoke solemnly in a half whisper.

'Do you know what it's like to lose your hair in your twenties?'

'No, sir,' said Matt and Rob in unison.

'No! No, you don't, do you . . . ?'

'We're only twelve, sir,' volunteered Matt.

'Don't be facetious!' snapped Pavey. 'I too once had lovely dark locks of hair not unlike your own, Mills,' he said, turning back to the bookcase and absentmindedly placing his hand on Matt's head. Matt flinched slightly and swallowed hard. This was weird!

'Lovely dark curly locks of hair that I was able to style in all sorts of ways. Yes! For a while I had a centre parting, then when the sixties came in and the fashion was for longer hair I let it grow down to cover my ears ...' As he said this he patted Matt's hair down over his ears as if it were his own. 'Sometimes I would comb it back ...' he jerked Matt's fringe back off his forehead, '... and other times I would brush it forward.' He smoothed Matt's hair back down over his forehead again, all the time looking at his own reflection in the glass door of the bookcase. 'I'd wash it and dry it, and other times I'd just look in the mirror and enjoy it!'

Suddenly Mr Pavey's mood changed from wistful to dark and brooding. 'Then one day it decided to leave me!'

He turned dramatically from the mirror to face the boys, his voice cracking with emotion. Matt and

Rob glanced briefly at each other – they were very nearly cracking up too but for a different reason.

'Oh, it started slowly at first,' said Pavey, staring into the middle distance. 'I would notice a few stray hairs on the pillow in the morning. When I styled it the comb would take more hair with it than it combed, then after a while I'd find whole clumps of my hair, my lovely dark curly hair, clogging up the plughole in the shower! I tried everything! Lotions, potions ... I combed the thick bit over the thin bit, I wore hats! For three months I spent an hour of every day standing on my head to increase the blood flow to my scalp.'

By now Matt and Rob were having to bite their tongues to stop themselves laughing, but still Pavey kept on.

'I even visited a doctor in a clinic in London who recommended an operation to remove the bald patch. I nearly went through with it too, but he told me there was a risk that it would make my ears go higher up the side of my head, so my glasses would be at an angle!'

Pavey stifled a sniffle and then let out an almost animal-like whine. 'Why ME?!' he wailed, sinking to his knees, and as he did so he pulled violently on Matt's fringe.

'Ouch!' yelped Matt.

Matt's cry seemed to startle Mr P out of his trance-like state. He looked across at his hand in

Matt's hair, hastily withdrew it and sprang to his feet.

'Ahem!' he said, clearing his throat and snapping back into headmaster mode. 'It's two weeks of detention for you two!'

He leant in close to them both again. '... And if I catch you up to any more shenanigans or you breathe a word of what I just said to anyone, you will be EXPELLED!'

Matt and Rob walked silently from the headmaster's office and didn't utter a word to each other until they reached the privacy of the boys' toilets, at which point ... they both burst out laughing.

'Can you believe that?!' said Matt with tears of laughter forming in his eyes. 'He was going to have an operation that would push his ears halfway up his head!'

'Hang on a sec!' said Rob and, pulling out a notepad, he started to draw a cartoon. When he'd finished he held it up for Matt to see. It showed Mr

Pavey with his ears on top of his head like Mickey Mouse. 'There's the new Pavey's Punchlines page!' he spluttered.

'No, mate,' said Matt, barely able to speak for laughing. 'That's not the page – that's the cover!'

14

A Brilliant Loser

'Well? How'd it go?' said Ian, looking up from his copy of *Mojo*.

'Brilliant!' said Matt, slinging his sports bag on to the couch and delving into the fridge for something to eat. The extreme ups and downs of the day had left him *very* hungry.

'Brilliant, eh? Hmm. So you won it, did you?' huffed Ian.

'Not exactly,' said Matt, grabbing a pork pie from the back of the fridge and examining its use-by date.

'Second?' asked Ian.

'Not second, no . . .'

'Third?'

'Not third either. Look, we were disqualified,' said Matt, taking a chunk out of the pork pie and looking in the cupboard for a packet of crisps. 'But it was SO cool.'

'Yeah, I heard,' said Ian coldly. 'It was SO cool in fact that the headmaster's office phoned me, and believe me, it wasn't to congratulate you on your comedy skills!'

'Ah,' said Matt, stopping mid-bite.

'Really, Matthew . . .'

'There he goes again,' thought Matt.

'It's just not fair!' growled Ian, slamming his magazine on to the coffee table. 'I've got enough to worry about without having to deal with phone calls from the school telling me my—'

'Stepson,' interjected Matt.

'. . . my stepson has insulted the headmaster! I was right in the middle of a viewing too!'

'Oh yes?' asked Matt facetiously. 'Anything nice?'

'As a matter of fact, yes, it's a lovely two-bedroom flat we've got on the market with a number of original features and patio – ideal for a newly married couple thinking of starting a family – but that's beside the point!' Ian shook his head forlornly and leaned towards Matt. 'When your mother headed off on her trip to Birmingham with the Dachshund Five, I promised her that for the three weeks she was away I'd look after you. The last thing I need is for her to get back to find you expelled from school!'

'I've got two weeks' detention, so not quite expelled. It'll actually make things easier for you, Ian – you won't see quite so much of me!'

'Good!' said Ian, then, realising what he'd said, he tried to correct himself. 'No! I mean ... er ... well ...'

'Don't worry, Ian, I know where I stand.'

'Now hang on, I didn't mean—' spluttered Ian, backtracking now, but Matt was already halfway up the stairs to his room.

15

The Kitty Hope Comedy Agency

The next day Matt and Rob were greeted like heroes everywhere they went. Even the teachers were giving them approving smiles and knowing looks. Mr Gillingham went so far as to take Matt to one side and tell him that he should have won. 'You're a very funny lad and a great communicator, and don't ever forget that, Matt. It's a gift you've got there and it'll set you up for life if you use it well.'

'You mean for good, sir?' said Matt cheekily. 'Rather than for evil?' and as he said this he contorted his face and body into something resembling Gollum from *The Lord of the Rings*. 'Filthy little hobbitses. They stole it from us. Wicked, tricksy, false!'

'Ha!' guffawed Mr Gillingham. 'Neil Trottman may be small but he's not quite a hobbit. I suggest you keep your head down for the rest of term as a certain someone has his eye on you.'

'Thanks, sir!' said Matt. Mr Gillingham nodded and wandered off with his pile of books to the next lesson. Why couldn't all the teachers be like him? thought Matt – interested, fun, inspiring.

Mr Pavey on the other hand had enjoyed every minute of cutting Matt and Rob down to size and this time there had been no neat escape. Their punishment was to stay after school and pick up litter around Anglebrook for two whole weeks.

'How's my number one client today?' said Rob, giving Matt a slap on the back. 'Seen this?' He held up his iPhone and touched the little white triangle floating in the middle of the screen. The title of the clip faded up: 'Matt Mills Owns Pavey'. What followed were edited highlights of Matt's takedown of Mr P set to the Tupac version of 'Every Breath You Take'.

'Blimey, if Pavey sees that we'll be back in for more flippin' detentions!' said Matt. 'What derr-brain stuck it on YouTube?'

'Me!' said Rob proudly. 'I did it last night. It's promotional. There's no such thing as bad publicity, remember?'

'Hmmm, that's not strictly true,' came a small voice from somewhere under their noses. Matt and Rob looked down to see a small girl, not quite four feet tall, with huge black-rimmed glasses and her hair cut in a tight black bob. She was holding a clipboard. 'Fame isn't quite the same thing as notoriety,' she continued, 'and a bad smell has a tendency to hang around.'

'She's right – you'd better take it down, Rob, and fast.'

'Hang on, who . . . ?' said Rob with a frown.

'Well done!' she said to Matt, ignoring Rob.

'Oh, er . . . thanks,' said Matt.

'You were funny, you should have won. Neil was good too but he's essentially a novelty act. Where does he go with it? The fact that he's tiny and looks like a bit of a nerd helps, but he's not going to look like that forever. No, he's got a short shelf life. It's you that everyone was talking about on the way home.'

'Well, fair play to Neil I guess . . .' said Matt, but she cut him off.

'I liked the gag about the optician. Is that one of yours?'

'Yes, but I'd never tried it before.'

'Everyone's talking about the Pavey takedown,' said Rob testily.

'Yes, I see that,' said the girl, ignoring Rob completely. 'The room was turning against you and you had to do something to bring it back round, so you picked on the head, but it was a bit cheap. The optician gag proves you can write, but you should have opened with it.'

'No, well, I was in a bit of a hole at the time – unfortunately Rob here had a bad case of the jitters.'

'Obviously you need to go solo,' she said, indicating Rob. 'He's holding you back.'

'I am here, you know!' said Rob, a note of irritation rising in his voice.

'I know he's your friend,' she went on, 'but there's

no room for sentiment – it's called show business, not show friendship.'

'Now hang on a sec!' said Rob.

But she wouldn't hang on, no, if anything she was beginning to hit her stride.

'There's more to a double act than just taking it in turns with the lines. There has to be a relationship – a funny man and a straight man. Always open with your best gag – close with your second best—'

'Hang on, hang on . . .' said Matt, holding up his hand in an attempt to get her to halt.

'Yes?' she said, blinking up at him through her specs.

'Sorry, do I know you?' asked Matt.

'Kitty Hope,' she said, handing Matt a business card.

KITTY HOPE
Personal Management

'Personal management?' said Matt with a smile.

'Yes, personal management. If you want to get somewhere in the entertainment business you need someone who's going to fight your corner, guide your career through the minefield of ... Why are you laughing?'

'Well, you're only about four!' chuckled Matt.

'Yeah! What time's the next train back to Lilliput?' chipped in Rob, nudging Matt in the ribs.

'Do you sleep in a slipper?' laughed Matt.

'Very good!' said Kitty, rolling her eyes skyward. 'I could milk a cow standing up, I'd make a great fridge magnet. I've heard them all before. You can do better than that. I'm eleven years old, I'm serious about management, and comedy is a serious business if you want to get on, but maybe you'd prefer to just play at it.'

She turned and started to walk off.

'No, hang on a sec,' said Matt. What she'd said had struck a chord. Kitty turned to face him, one hand on her hip, the other clutching her precious clipboard.

'He's got a manager,' butted in Rob firmly. 'Me!'

'Now that's the best joke I've heard all day,' she said.

'Listen, Kitty,' said Matt, taking a couple of paces towards her. 'I appreciate the interest but I'm sorted for management so . . .'

'Whatever! If you change your mind, call me. You've got real talent, Matt Mills, you could be big and I'd really like to be involved.'

And with that this eleven-year-old, three-foot-six dynamo strode off, clipboard under her arm.

16

Peaks and Troughs

The warm glow from 'Anglebrook's Got Talent' lasted Matt for a couple of days and then he started to get restless. He wanted that feeling again. The natural high you get from performing live. He'd only done one gig but he was hooked.

'Hey, Mr Manager!' he said, bounding up to Rob in first break in their usual meeting place outside the science block. 'How are the gigs coming along? Anything for the diary?'

'Oh hi, Matt,' said Rob, shifting uneasily from one foot to the other. 'Bit difficult that, because there aren't really any comedy clubs nearby, are there?'

'S'pose not,' said Matt. He hadn't really expected anything different. He'd asked Rob a few times and the answer was always the same – nothing doing. In Matt's mind Rob was his manager and he expected him to actually try and get him some gigs, but it seemed that as far as Rob was concerned it was more of an honorary role.

'Couldn't you, like, organise a gig?' said Matt hopefully.

'Organise one?' said Rob, a little surprised. 'How?'

'Well, you know, maybe phone up a pub or . . .'

'We're only twelve, Matt!' said Rob. 'We wouldn't even get through the door!'

'Well, how about a theatre or a talent night somewhere?'

'Yeah, I suppose I could. To be honest I've been really busy with my art project. We're doing portraits, we've got a trip planned up to London to the Tate Modern, it's gonna be epic!'

'Oh,' said Matt mournfully. 'Did you get a reply from *The T Factor*?' he asked hopefully.

The T Factor was the country's foremost TV talent show.

'You have to be sixteen for that,' said Rob. 'That's been the main problem, Matt, there just doesn't seem to be a comedy circuit for our age group.'

Matt shrugged and kicked a loose piece of paving down the steps into the playground.

'I don't think I can wait, mate,' he said. 'If I've got to hang around for another four years before I can get a gig I think I'll go mad. There must be another way to get some stage time.'

'All right, I'll have another think. Leave it with me,' said Rob.

'What are you thinking?' said Matt, ever the optimist. 'I know that look, Browny, you're up to something.'

'Don't get your hopes up,' said Rob, holding up his hands and backing away from Matt. 'I've got an idea, that's all, an outside chance.'

As the bell rang Matt contemplated his lot. Double physics followed by double maths, a horrible school dinner, the promise of an hour picking up litter and the whole lot rounded off by an evening spent with an estate agent. From where he was standing, it didn't look good. It didn't look good at all.

17

The Big Time

The next day, it was Rob's turn to bound up to Matt at the school gates. He looked really excited.

'Hey, Matt! You're not going to believe this!' he gushed.

'Try me,' said Matt, still pretty depressed about his circumstances.

'I've got you a gig!'

'What?!' said Matt, grabbing Rob by the lapels of his jacket. 'This had better not be a wind-up! I don't think I could take it!'

'Straight up. A stand-up gig – and get this – you get paid too!'

'Paid?! Paid?!! Like real money!?'

Rob nodded enthusiastically.

'B-b-but . . . where?'

'The Biddleden Women's Institute Annual Cheese and Wine Party!'

'I said don't wind me up!' said Matt, letting go of Rob, shoving his hands in his pockets and marching off towards assembly.

'Hey, hear me out!' said Rob, chasing after him.

'The Women's Institute?!' cried Matt. 'I'll die on my . . . !'

'Listen to me!' said Rob, grabbing Matt's shoulders and turning him round to face him. 'You've got it wrong! You're thinking the WI is just a whole load of old ladies who like knitting and baking cakes and don't know the first thing about humour, when in fact—'

'They're a whole load of old ladies who like knitting and baking cakes and don't know the first thing about humour,' said Matt.

'No, some of them are under fifty!'

'Whoopee-doo! Maybe I'll pick up a girlfriend there too!' Matt said, shaking free of Rob's grasp and walking on.

'A gig's a gig!' Rob shouted after him.

Matt stopped dead. Rob had a point. What was the alternative? To cling on to his one moment of glory at the school talent show? A show that he actually entered as a double act, got away with by making it up as he went along, then ended up being disqualified? He thought back to the laughs and applause he'd got that day. If that was how it went when he was ad libbing, think how great it could be if he had a proper, prepared stand-up act. Rob was right, a gig was a gig.

'Where do I have to be, and how long do I have to do?'

'That's my boy!' said Rob, running to catch him up. 'Stick with me and we'll soon have you at the Apollo! The Cheese and Wine Party at the WI is just the beginning.'

'Sure, I can see myself playing old people's homes and intensive care units! Funeral parlours!'

'Hey, you two jokers! Mills and Brown! Get in here now!' It was Mr Avery in his tracksuit.

'I'll see you on the steps at first break,' said Rob as they both jogged towards the site of their last success, the assembly hall.

18

Say Cheese

It turned out the so-called gig was in two days'
time at 4.30 p.m. at the Parish Rooms in the nearby
village of Biddleden, in front of sixty members of the
Women's Institute. Matt was invited to do a fifteen-
minute spot. His payment would be his bus fare and
as much cheese and 'nibbles' as he could eat.

'Some manager Rob turned out to be,' thought
Matt. 'I'm the only stand-up being paid in
pounds – of cheese.' He fished in his pocket for
his little black book and wrote 'Paid in Cheese'.
That might be the start of a nice little routine
for the good ladies of Biddleden. Stage time was

stage time and what would he be doing on Friday at 4.30 otherwise? Oh yes – picking up litter for Mr Pavey. Ouch! It looked very much like he had a double-booking. He'd need to find an ingenious way out of his detention.

> ## PAID IN CHEESE : SLIDING SCALE OF PAYMENTS.
>
> 5-minute set – Dairylea Triangle
> 10-minute set – 2 cheesestrings
> 20-minute set – Big ball of Edam
> 40-minute (extended) set – Full cheeseboard

'There's no way he'll think I'm you, bruv,' protested Ahmed at first break. 'I'm a different colour for a start!'

'That's just a detail,' said Matt, trying to calm Ahmed down. 'Listen, you wear my hoody pulled right up over your face.'

'What about my hands?'

'You wear gloves.'

'It's ridiculous! If I get caught I won't need to pretend I'm on litter-picking detention because I actually will be – most likely for the rest of term!'

'Trust me, you won't get caught. Once you report for duty they just leave you alone.'

'But I don't sound anything like you!'

'Just put on a hoarse voice and if he asks tell him you've got a sore throat.'

'What's in it for me? Why should I put my neck on the line just so you can do this poxy cheese show?'

'It's not a cheese show, it's a gig at a cheese and wine— Look, we're friends, right?'

Ahmed nodded.

'You want me to succeed in stand-up comedy, right?'

'Well, kind of . . . but not if it means my own life is over!'

'Imagine the stories you'll have when I get famous. People will be saying, "Did you see Matt Mills on TV last night?" and you'll be able to say, "Yeah I went to school with him, as a matter of fact, I helped him on his way."'

'Yeah, as I wait tables in McDonald's because I was expelled from school.'

'Oh come on, Ahmed.'

'Nah, sorry, bruv, can't help you.' Ahmed turned to walk away.

'I'll split the fee with you, after management commission!'

'Management commission!' said Ahmed incredulously. 'You've got a manager?!'

'Yeah, Rob's doing it – well, for the time being.'

'You must be bonkers giving him any cash. All right, I tell you what, we split the payment fifty–fifty and you got a deal.'

'Done!' said Matt, shaking Ahmed's hand.

For the rest of the day Matt's teachers might have thought that he was paying perfect attention to their lessons – he was facing the front and his eyes appeared to be trained on the work in hand – but behind those eyes his mind was racing, plotting, planning, refining the fifteen minutes he'd be doing at the Biddleden Parish Rooms.

'Hi, girls!' – No, that was too informal – 'Good afternoon, ladies!' – No, too polite. How about a simple 'Hello'? Yes, 'Hello, Biddleden!' Yes, that was more like it. Maybe he could put on a voice like a rock star greeting a packed Wembley Stadium. 'Hello, BIDDLEDEEEEEEN!' Then what? He scanned the pages of his little black book, which he'd hidden under his exercise book. 'I haven't seen so many women over fifty in one place since . . . since . . . hmmm,' he thought, what was something where you'd see a load of older women? A funeral? – Bit creepy! Marks & Spencer – yes! That was it. 'I haven't seen so many women over fifty since Marks & Spencer had a sale on cardigans!' he chuckled to himself. He was off.

'What's so funny, Mr Mills?' came the stern voice of Dr Bouvier, the physics teacher, dragging Matt back into the here and now.

'Huh?' said Matt, slightly confused to find himself in a physics lesson.

'You were laughing. Perhaps you'd like to share your joke with the class?'

'Oh, well . . .' said Matt, playing for time. 'Um, it

was a science-related joke, sir!'

'Oh really?' said Bouvier, sitting forward, suddenly interested. 'Continue.'

'Um . . .' Matt racked his brains to try and recall what little physics he actually knew. Then the spark of an idea fired up. 'What do you call a bunch of atoms that live underground, sir?'

'This doesn't sound very promising,' said Bouvier, 'but tell me anyway.'

'No, sir, you have to repeat the question in your answer – you know, like you told us to do in exams?'

There was a smattering of titters from around the class.

Dr Bouvier frowned.

'Very well, I don't know, what DO you call a bunch of atoms that live underground?'

'A *mole*-cule.'

There was silence in the classroom. You could hear a pin drop – in fact you could hear a pin falling. In fact you could hear a pin just being a pin. Then it started, a weird barking noise.

MOLE-CULE

'HONG! HONG! HONG! HONG! HONG! HONG!!' It was Dr Bouvier. He was laughing. 'HONG! HONG! HONG! HONG! HONG! HONG!!' he went and the class started laughing too – not at the joke but at Dr Bouvier. No one had ever heard him laugh before. It was like a cross between a seal and a vintage car. The more he laughed, the more they laughed. The more they laughed the more Dr Bouvier laughed. 'Sir, I think I've just created a chain reaction!' said Matt, as the bell rang for the end of the lesson. He slung his physics textbook into his sports bag and sprinted for the door, leaving his teacher and the rest of his class in stitches.

BIDDLEDEN WI SET LIST

- Hello, Biddleden (like at the O2)
- Make some noise
- Electric lights
- Twinned with itself
- Town motto
- White lines
- Postcards
- Light bulb
- Duck pond
- Tippex on computer
- Cakes
- Bake Off (Mary Berry stuff)
- What are the men doing?
- Grey hair stuff (squirrel)
- OAP Rap
- Goodnight

19

The Gig of the Century

'Heeeelllllloooooo, Biddddddllledeeen!' bellowed Matt to his own reflection in the mirror in the boys' toilets at half past three on the day of the gig. He looked at his set list, then at the hairbrush he was using as a microphone and slung it into the sink. He was having a job convincing *himself* he was a stand-up comic – let alone a room full of members of the Women's Institute.

He looked again at the bus times for Biddleden on his smartphone. There was one in the morning – which didn't appear to come back – and another in twenty minutes which did.

He'd been a little nervous at the talent show but this was different, it was a completely unknown quantity. He didn't know exactly where the venue was, what it looked like, how it was set up – and he certainly didn't know whether his act would appeal to the women who were attending. He could feel that tight knot in his stomach again, his mouth was a little bit dry and he felt slightly zoned out from the rest of the world – there was no room in his brain for anything other than the gig. He adjusted his suit and tie and took one last look at himself in the mirror. Staring back at him was what looked like a stand-up comedian. Suddenly a sense of calm descended – the day had arrived, the gig was finally happening and if he wasn't ready now, he'd never be. Matt smiled and winked at his reflection. 'Right, let's get to work!' he said, and turned to high-five his mate, but Rob wasn't there. He had planned to accompany Matt to the gig in his capacity as manager but it had coincided with his art trip to London.

It dawned on Matt that he had no one to lean on, no one to share the trip to the gig with, and more importantly no one to blame if it didn't go well. He gathered up his little black book and his set list and headed off for the delights of Biddleden.

To call Biddleden a one-horse town would be an insult to horses. It was more of a one-goat town. It had a post office with combined mini-mart and

(ONE-GOAT TOWN)

a pub – and that was it. Even the mobile library didn't stop there, in fact it sped up as it approached the place. The one thing it did have, however, was a thriving Women's Institute for whom the annual Cheese and Wine Party was the highlight of the year.

'Welcome to the Biddleden Parish Rooms, I'm Margaret Hudd and you must be Master Mills the entertainer!' said a tiny elderly lady with white hair and a Zimmer frame at the front door of the venue.

'Stand-up comic really,' said Matt, shaking her hand. 'Call me Matt. I like the sign!' He nodded towards the large handwritten poster stuck to the front of her Zimmer frame showing details of the Cheese and Wine Party.

'Yes, well, it pays to advertise!' she said gamely.

'That's right,' thought Matt. 'If you sell out tonight I can see you being offered the Nike advertising account.'

He suddenly had a picture in his head of hundreds of old ladies in Nike trainers dancing with Zimmer frames to a Jay Z track.

'We are terribly excited this year because the regional head of the Women's Institute is coming all the way from Stonebridge Wells to be with us, so we're really hoping to make a big impression,' said Margaret, showing Matt to his dressing room.

'Oh, no pressure then,' Matt thought. 'Just the regional head of the WI and she's come a full twenty miles, all the way from Stonebridge Wells!'

'What was the entertainment last year?' he asked.

'It was quite wonderful!' said Margaret. 'It was

Ken Styles, a gentleman from Hambridge who folded balloons into the shape of birds and mammals commonly seen in the Kent region. His squirrel was uncannily realistic, and his badger too, but what really brought the house down was his rook! Amazing to be able to capture the grace of one of God's creatures just by folding some balloons, don't you think?'

'Um, yes, absolutely,' said Matt.

'We tried to book him again this year but the Rotary Club got in early and gazumped us. He's terribly popular locally.'

'I can imagine!' said Matt. 'An act like that must be like gold dust.'

'Quite so,' agreed Margaret, Matt's sarcasm flying over her head and through a small stained-glass window.

'Well, here we are!' she said, indicating a door with the words 'Ken Styles' written on it. 'Oops! No one's used it since last year!' she said. 'I'll leave you to prepare. Let me know if you need anything.'

With that she started to shuffle back towards the front door.

'There is something I need ...' muttered Matt under his breath. 'A new manager!'

He looked around his dressing room. There was a high window with frosted glass and in one corner there was a sink.

'Pwor! What's that smell?' he muttered. Then he saw it. Next to the sink was a small table piled high with cheese. 'Yuk! Who has a whole evening based around cheese?'

He studied his set list. At that moment none of it looked in the least bit funny.

'Ready to go?' said Margaret, turning up at his door ten minutes later.

Matt stood and nodded. He took a swig of orange squash. 'Dead man walking,' he muttered and headed for the stage.

A rather severe-looking woman with a powdered face, horn-rimmed spectacles and hair in a bun was on stage wrapping up her talk on 'The History of the Sponge Cake'. '... And it's still one of the most popular cakes in Britain today!' she said, finishing to rapturous applause.

'Follow that!' she hissed at Matt as she passed him waiting in the wings.

Margaret had taken the stage clutching a Post-it note with Matt's introduction on it. 'Well, I'm sure you'd like to join with me in thanking Janet Breadstick for a most illuminating speech. I think you'll agree we'll never look at a sponge cake in the same way again!' she said with a broad smile. Another round of applause rang out. 'Now, we all remember last year the gentleman from Hambridge who folded balloons into the shape of birds and mammals commonly seen in the Kent region ...' There were loud cries of 'Yes!' and 'Hambridge!' and even a few claps.

'Blimey!' thought Matt. 'He's getting a round of applause and he's not even here!'

'His squirrel was uncannily realistic,' Margaret

went on, warming to the theme, 'and his badger, well, it was out of this world . . .'

There were widespread mutterings of agreement.

'Not to mention his rook!'

Another ripple of applause.

'Is he back again this year?' came a lone voice from the third row.

'No, no he's not.'

Matt's audience let out a loud groan of disappointment.

'No, I'm afraid the Rotary Club got there first.'

There were loud cries of 'Boo!' and 'Down with the Rotary Club!'

'Ladies, please!' said Margaret, tapping the microphone loudly to get their attention. Eventually they quietened down.

'Thank you! The balloon-folder from Hambridge couldn't make it. However, we are very pleased to welcome a young boy from neighbouring Staplefirst . . .'

'Oooh!' went the crowd of older ladies and Matt

could hear them repeating the word 'Staplefirst' as if Staplefirst was on the other side of the world.

'Please give a lovely warm Women's Institute welcome to Matt Milk!'

'Matt Milk?' exclaimed Matt in dismay. 'Matt *Milk?*'

This was turning into the gig of the century.

The warm Women's Institute welcome consisted of the sort of applause you hear at a cricket match when the sun comes out after it's been raining.

Matt bounded on to the stage.

'Heeeelllllooooooo, Biddddddllleden!' he said, to complete silence. He tried again. 'I said, Hello, Biddleden!'

'What did he say?' said someone from up the back.

Undeterred, Matt pressed on.

'Greetings from Staplefirst where we have electric lights! Wow, I'm finally in Biddleden! Such a quiet town it's actually twinned with itself!'

The silence continued unbroken.

'Biddleden! Whose village motto is "Biddleden – we have a pond!"'

Still nothing.

'Such a small town that when they painted the white lines they had to widen the road first. So small, the picture postcards are blank!'

Still nothing, just the gentle clicking of new dentures.

'Hello? This is weird, I'm saying lots of really funny things into this microphone but something happens to them as they come out of the speakers!' said Matt with a big grin. Still nothing. Talk about a tough crowd – this was like wading through peanut butter.

The ladies of Biddleden shifted uneasily in their seats. Matt pressed on.

'Rumour has it that a light bulb blew in the post office three years ago and it made the front page of the *Biddleden Gazette*!'

Starting to panic, Matt broke one of the first rules of live stand-up – he started to speed up.

RULES OF STAND-UP

1. If the audience are proving tough, don't speed up. This makes it harder for them to hear you, and ruins your comic timing. If anything you should slow down.

2. Be consistent to your comedy persona. Even the most straightfoward comic has a persona or character, which is often an exaggeration of themselves. If you come out of your persona the audience spot it straight away and it reminds them they're watching an act.

3. Don't force it. It needs to look effortless. There's nothing worse than the comic who's trying too

hard. It's the difference between comic and tragic.

4. If it works, keep it in. If it doesn't, throw it out. Acts tend to evolve rather than be written in one go.

5. After your gig, when it's still fresh in your mind, go back through your set list and remind yourself what went well and what went not so well.

6. If a gig goes badly, try to understand why but don't obsess about it, suck it up and move on.

'I passed the mayor of Biddleden trying to get rid of his reflection in the duck pond with a rake! Hey, did you hear about the bloke from Biddleden who tried to delete his emails and ended up with Tippex on his computer screen?'

'What'd he say?' came a voice from up the back.

The speed of Matt's delivery made it even more difficult for the ladies of Biddleden to follow his gags and any comic timing he may have had quickly evaporated.

The general unease now escalated to fidgeting and full-scale muttering. Matt looked down to see one lady reach into her bag for her knitting. 'Hey, I hear knitting is really big in the WI?' he said, breaking out of the routine for a moment.

One or two of the ladies stopped talking and looked at him with something approaching interest.

'My nan actually got her hair caught in her knitting and ended up inside a balaclava she can't take off!' There were a couple of audible tuts as Matt acted out his joke, trying to pull off an imaginary balaclava that was stuck to his head. The lady in the front row with the knitting needles took that as a cue to start knitting. By now Matt's throat was as dry as a Ryvita in a wind tunnel.

At that point a large lady in a felt hat with a piece of netting over her face walked in and everyone turned round to look at her.

'I can't just ignore her!' thought Matt, and before he'd realised what he'd said he'd shot out one of his best heckle put-downs: 'Is that a moustache, luv, or have your eyebrows come down for a drink?'

The audience gasped as one.

The lady in the hat looked extremely angry but Matt pressed on with his heckle put-downs.

'Is that your real face or are you still celebrating Halloween?'

Another gasp.

'Who does your make-up when the circus leaves town?'

This time there was a stifled scream.

'I've never been so insulted in all my life!' said the

lady in the hat.

'Oh, why don't you freeze your teeth and give your tongue a sleigh ride!' said Matt. 'Perhaps you'd like to stand up and tell the class a bit about yourself?'

Most of the 'class' were busy shrinking into their seats with embarrassment.

Margaret appeared at the side of the stage and started to shuffle towards Matt. As she reached him she prised the microphone out of his sweaty palm and spoke.

'There's no need for her to introduce herself, we all know very well who she is – this lady is the regional head of the WI and has come all the way from Stonebridge Wells!'

Matt bit his lip. He wished the ground would open and swallow him up. He'd thought that picking up litter was humiliating but it was nothing compared to this!

The lady in the hat charged up to the front of the stage and fixed Matt with a very angry stare. 'My name is Mrs Phillida Pavey. I think you might know

my husband. Stand up, Meredith!' she crowed.

Sure enough, at the back of the hall, like the sun rising in the morning, up popped the shiny bald bonce of Mr Pavey.

'So, Mr Mills . . .' he said, his big fat tongue lolling out and wetting his lips. 'We meet again!'

20

Just Deserts

'Take a seat, Mr Mills,' said Mr Pavey, sitting behind his desk and cracking his knuckles.

'Actually it's Woodwood – like two planks of wood?' said Ian, sitting back in the plush leather chair opposite Mr Pavey's desk. He looked across at Matt sitting in the hard wooden chair next to him.

'I'm sorry?' said Mr Pavey with a frown.

'I'm the boy's stepfather, not—'

'Quite so,' interrupted Mr P. 'Now, you're no doubt wondering why I've called you in to see me today.'

'Well, I'm guessing it's something to do with young Matthew here,' said Ian, sinking further into his seat.

'Indeed it is,' said Mr Pavey, standing and walking over to the window.

'Here we go ...' thought Matt, bracing himself.

Pavey took a deep breath and turned to face them both.

'It seems to me we have before us, Mr Plank, a boy who is completely obsessed with acting the fool and trying to make people laugh.'

'Tell me about it!' said Ian, visibly relaxing – he'd never liked this bald bloke with the glasses but now at least they had something in common. 'All I hear about is stand-up comedians!' he said, nodding his head in agreement.

'The boy shows very little interest in anything but stand-up comedy,' said Pavey, 'and I'm afraid to say I caught him dodging his detention so that he could entertain the ladies of the Biddleden Women's Institute ...'

'Strewth!' said Ian, rolling his eyes. 'I bet they're a bunch of dragons.'

'Of which my wife is the Regional Head!' continued Pavey.

'Ah, yes, well,' said Ian, backtracking wildly, 'er . . . how was the show?'

'I have to tell you that to a man the ladies found it thoroughly offensive and not in the least bit funny!' said Pavey.

'Ah well, there you go,' said Ian, turning to Matt. 'What have I been telling you, Matthew? You're wasting your time. See, traditionally the best comedians come from the north . . .'

'I, however,' interjected Mr Pavey, 'found young Matt's discourse on life from the perspective of a young lad growing up in rural Kent hilarious!'

'What did he just say?!' thought Matt, shaking his head. He could have sworn Mr Pavey had just said he thought his act was hilarious.

'Offering as it did some brilliant observations on the vagaries of the Women's Institute! Vagaries that

I know only too well.' Pavey's face broke into an enormous grin. 'That bunch of do-gooders deserved it!' he said, thumping the table with his fist. 'I've wanted to say half those things for years! Ha ha! From the mouths of babes, eh, Mr Plank?'

'It's Woodwood actually,' said Ian.

'You must be very proud, Mr Woodplank!' gushed Mr Pavey, barely pausing for breath. 'The most impressive part was that he stuck to his guns! Even though the ladies of the WI weren't the least bit amused, Matt here didn't pander to them – and neither should he! His material was brilliantly inventive! I predict a big future for him!'

'Well, I ... er ... I s'pose so ...' mumbled Ian, rather confused – was his stepson in trouble or not?

Then Pavey turned to Matt. 'Congratulations!' he said, shaking him by the hand.

'Yes, exactly what I said!' said Ian. It was finally dawning on him that Matt wasn't going to get expelled. 'I suppose he gets a lot of it from me, I've always been one for a joke. Did you hear the one about the mother-in-law who went to the zoo . . .'

But Mr Pavey wasn't listening to Ian.

'Did you write it all yourself, Matt?' he asked.

'Um, yeah, um . . .' Matt really didn't know what to make of the situation.

'Of course, humour has been used to great effect in literature,' continued Mr Pavey. 'Take Shakespeare's comedies, Chaucer . . . I thought at times your monologue had echoes of the great Jonathan Swift.'

'Aren't you annoyed that I . . . ?' Matt stuttered.

'That you bunked off school? Ordinarily, yes, and don't make a habit of it, but it was worth it just to see Mrs P's face. Priceless! Good luck to you, Matt.'

He reached into his desk drawer and retrieved a very old tin. 'Here, have a toffee. I'm going to be keeping a close eye on your career from now on!'

'No toffee for me?' asked Ian hopefully.

'I'm not made of toffees, Mr Woodworm!' said Mr Pavey, ushering them out of his office. 'Oh, and Matt?'

'Yes, Mr Pavey?'

'Don't worry about the litter-picking next week!'

'Yeah?' said Matt brightening.

'No, instead spend the time writing some more jokes!'

Matt pinched himself again, then stamped on his own feet – first his left, then his right.

'What ARE you doing?' said Ian.

'Making sure I'm not dreaming!' said Matt, popping the toffee into his mouth. He spat it straight back out into his hand. 'Yuk! That's got more fluff on it than Pavey's head!'

'Look, I don't know what that was all about, I'm sure,' said Ian with a note of irritation in his voice, 'but try and keep your nose clean. I missed two viewings for this! Just wait till your mother gets home from the Midlands.'

Matt watched as Ian headed towards the exit. Then his eye was caught by one of the coats on the pegs outside Mr Pavey's office. It was moving! Two legs dropped down from inside it and out poked the face of Rob Brown.

'He called you Matt!' said Rob incredulously, his eyes almost popping out of his head. 'What's going on?'

'Not only that, Rob, he gave me a toffee!' said Matt, opening his hand to reveal the ancient sweet. 'It's a long story. But before we get to that I need to talk to you about how to set up a comedy gig.'

'Hey, look, it's my twin brother!' said Ahmed, wandering up to meet them.

'Oh man! I almost forgot!' said Matt, slapping his forehead with the palm of his hand. 'How'd it go?'

'No problem, bruv! I turned up with the hoody and the gloves, said I had a sore throat like you told me, and Mr Avery even offered me a Strepsil!'

'Sweeeeeeet!' said Matt, laughing.

'How was the gig?'

'Put simply, it was the gig from hell. The audience were so tough it was like performing in an above-ground cemetery. On top of that I ended up dissing the headmaster's wife.'

'Jeez, that's bad.'

'Oh, Ahmed, while I've got you,' said Matt, fumbling about in his pocket. He withdrew a large piece of Cheddar cheese and slapped it into Ahmed's hand. 'There's your commission!'

21

An Unfortunate Truth

The next day Rob and Matt sat opposite each other in Greggs the bakers, each nursing a lukewarm cup of tea.

Matt ran through the entire debacle of the Biddleden WI gig and how it had been wrong in so many ways – the sound, the lighting – the audience – the cheese! He also explained how close he'd come to being expelled and about Mr Pavey's sudden conversion to being his number one fan.

'I don't get it,' said Rob. 'He hated your act at the talent show.'

'Yes, but that's because he was the butt of the jokes – when it was his wife I was taking the mick out of, he found it funny. There's a lesson there for me.'

'Yeah? What's that?'

'You never know who might be in the audience,' said Matt. 'Have you got me any other gigs?'

Rob toyed awkwardly with his teaspoon. 'Not exactly . . .' he said.

'Er, Rob, it's not really working with you as my manager, is it?' said Matt.

Rob shook his head and emptied another sachet of sugar into his cup. 'I guess not. The thing is I'm really enjoying my art at the moment – the trip to Tate Modern yesterday was just brilliant – there was this Damien Hirst piece – a real dead shark in a tank – so cool!'

'Yeah, I think I met her at my gig too,' joked Matt.

'Mr Sweeney reckons I could get into art school

if I stick at it, so every spare moment I get I need to work on my portfolio.'

'Hmmm. Well, I'm afraid, Rob, in the words of Alan Sugar – you're fired!'

'Really?'

'Really.'

Suddenly Rob relaxed and a smile came to his lips. 'Phew!' he said. 'I thought you were going to make me organise another gig!'

'So you didn't want to be my manager anyway?' said Matt.

'Don't get me wrong, I did quite enjoy it. Well, I enjoyed telling people I was your manager,' said Rob, 'but all that phoning round and negotiating your contract stuff . . .'

'I was paid in cheese.'

'Yeah, you've got a point.'

'Look, it's OK. It's my fault,' said Matt, shaking his head. 'You're right, you're an artist, you should concentrate on your art.'

'Oh yes, on that score I've got some good news,'

said Rob, brightening. 'You know I've got to do a portrait for my end-of-term project? Well, guess who's agreed to sit for me?'

'Rihanna?'

'Better than Rihanna!' said Rob, grinning like Phillip Schofield in a toothpaste commercial.

'If it's Mrs Pavey you'll need to get some more paint because she's . . .'

'Magda Avery!'

'Never!' said Matt, feeling a sudden pang of jealousy.

'Oh yes! On the condition that I give the picture to Dave Joy!'

'Sweet! You jammy wotsit . . .'

'Yeah, I'm going to be spending a lot of time with the hottest girl in the school!'

'Well, call me if you need anyone to wash your brushes for you.'

'Seriously, Matt,' said Rob. 'You need someone who really wants the job of managing you – who's as keen on comedy and knows as much about it as you.'

Matt got up to head back to school. 'Oh, I almost forgot,' he said. 'I got you a leaving present.'

'Yeah?' said Rob with a big smile.

'Yeah,' said Matt, slamming something wet and sticky into Rob's hand. 'It's an antique.'

Rob looked at the brown, sticky mess in his hand. It appeared to be a very old, furry, half-eaten toffee.

22

Homework Can Be Fun

Matt found her in the library, reading a copy of the *Stage*. 'I . . . er . . .' he began.

'Take a seat, I've been expecting you,' said Kitty Hope, her eyes fixed on her newspaper.

'I've been thinking about your offer,' said Matt.

'And?' said Kitty brusquely.

'I've changed my mind, I'd like you to manage me – if you're still up for it, that is.'

'I'm very glad to hear that,' said Kitty, finally looking up to meet Matt's gaze. She was beaming from ear to ear. 'How does Rob feel about it?

'He took it pretty well. He wasn't really enjoying it, to be honest.'

'Good. Well, let's get right down to business.' She reached into her bag and retrieved a large padded envelope. 'Here's your homework,' she said. 'In there you'll find DVDs of some of the best stand-up comedians that have ever lived – Richard Pryor, Joan Rivers, Billy Connolly, Tommy Cooper, Woody Allen, Eddie Murphy, Jo Brand, Jack Dee, Stewart Lee, Alexei Sayle,

Arnold Brown, Chris Rock, Bill Hicks, French and Saunders, Rik Mayall and Ade Edmondson, and my favourite – Harry Hill! Study them. Don't steal from them. Be inspired by what's possible when you break the rules.'

'You knew I'd change my mind, didn't you?' said Matt, taking the envelope and peering in at the handwritten labels.

'I had a pretty good idea,' she said.

'Will I need to sign a contract or … ?' asked Matt, suddenly feeling that the tables had been turned – that he was the junior partner in this new relationship, not her.

'No need,' said Kitty. 'All the time I'm doing a good job for you, why would you want to leave? No, I'll be happy with a handshake. Now do your homework. I'll meet you here tomorrow at morning break. Bring your diary – we're going to make a plan.'

'Sure thing,' said Matt, turning to leave. 'Um … I don't actually have a diary.'

'There's one on your phone.'

'Oh yeah. Cheers!' Matt headed for the library door.

'And before you go, Matt . . .'

He turned to see her with her arm outstretched for a handshake. He walked back, took her hand and shook it vigorously.

'Welcome to the Kitty Hope Comedy Agency!' she said with a grin.

23

A Human Being After All

'What's this tripe?' moaned Ian, pouring himself a tumbler of whisky and plonking himself down on the sofa.

'It's Eddie Izzard,' said Matt. Eddie's DVD was the first one that had fallen out of Kitty's envelope.

EDDIE IZZARD FACT FILE

Background: Started as a street performer

Style: Improvisational, surreal, rambling, stream of consciousness

'Darth Vader going to a Death Star canteen ...? What is he going on about? And what in God's name is he wearing?'

'He's a comedian who happens to be a transvestite,' said Matt.

'Reminds me of your auntie Jennie when she hasn't shaved,' said Ian. It was rather an unkind comment but it caused Matt to do something he'd never done before in response to one of Ian's witticisms – he laughed.

'That's pretty good – for you,' said Matt, chuckling and reaching for his little black book.

'I have my moments,' said Ian.

'Ian? Can I ask you a question?' Matt said, having

scribbled the line in his book.

'Depends ... is this one of your jokes?' said Ian warily. The ease with which they were suddenly getting on was a little unsettling for both of them.

'The other morning you said you hadn't always wanted to be an estate agent – is that true?'

'Ha!' said Ian. 'No one *wants* to be an estate agent! No one sits at school dreaming of trying to sell houses! It's just something you end up doing. Do you think I enjoy meeting a complete stranger outside a block of flats, showing them round a dump and trying to persuade them that it's the equivalent of Downton Abbey? Well, actually I do enjoy it as it happens, but it's not part of some great plan, no. No, I'll let you into a little secret. I was in a band as a teenager, with some mates. That's what I really wanted to do.'

'What?!' said Matt, sitting up, all ears. 'Wait a minute, you were in a boy band?' He was already imagining Ian and four other middle-aged, overweight blokes with thinning hair, perched on bar stools Westlife-style, singing 'Raise Me Up'.

'Do you mind!' said Ian. 'We were a punk band – Dead Toys, we were called.'

'Yeah? What instrument did you play?' asked Matt.

'Drums,' said Ian, grabbing a couple of pencils and beating out a few drum breaks on the coffee table. 'I've still got a kit set up at my mum's house. We played quite a few gigs actually, mainly local stuff, friends' parties, stuff like that. I had a safety pin through my nose and everything.'

'You?! Had a . . . piercing?!' exclaimed Matt, more than a little gobsmacked.

'Yeah, look!' said Ian, leaning in to Matt's face and pulling his nose to one side. Sure enough, Matt could see a small white scar above his left nostril.

'You? A p-p-punk rocker?' said Matt. 'I never would have believed it!'

'Yeah, it was a great laugh. The others wanted to carry on after we left school but the fashions changed – the New Romantics came in, it was over as soon as it began, and to be honest I couldn't see it paying my bills. A bloke in a pub told me about a job at the estate agent's and I just drifted into that. Don't get me wrong, it's not so bad, but I do sometimes wonder – what if?'

Eddie Izzard had just finished a routine about being brought up by Wolves – not the animals – the Wolverhampton Wanderers football team.

'Dear oh dear! You must have something better than this!' said Ian, picking Kitty's envelope up off the coffee table and sorting through Matt's homework DVDs. 'Ah, here we are – Billy Connolly, now he *is* a funny man.' Ian leant forward and loaded the DVD into its little tray.

Billy Connolly Fact File

- Background: Started as a folk singer and developed his stand-up from links between songs

- Style: Scottish, observational, earthy, ribald (a bit rude)

Nickname: The Big Yin

Influences: Monty Python

Top gag: joke about a man who murdered his wife and buried her bottom-up so he'd have somewhere to park his bike!

Homework: An Audience with Billy Connolly (1985)

Two minutes later they were both convulsed on the sofa in hysterics.

'See what I mean?!' guffawed Ian. 'The man's a genius! How can he turn farting into comedy gold?'

'My go!' said Matt once the Billy Connolly DVD had finished.

'Eh?' said Ian.

'You chose that one, now it's my turn. Get your laughing gear round this.' He selected Micky Flanagan's live tour show, loaded it up and pressed Play.

They both spent the next hour laughing their socks off. 'All right!' said Ian. 'I'll let you have that one!'

Just then Ian's phone sparked into life and on the screen appeared the face of Matt's mum, Jenny.

'Hello, gorgeous!' said Ian.

'Yuk!' moaned Matt. This sort of talk between his mum and his stepdad turned his stomach.

'How's it going, Snoopy?'

'Snoopy?' muttered Matt. Wasn't Snoopy a cartoon dog with black ears, a long nose and very short legs?

'Hmmm, now you come to mention it there are similarities,' he thought, reaching for his little black book. 'Idea – Pet Names', he wrote. 'Number 1: Snoopy.'

'Yes, he's here, we've been watching DVDs together,' cooed Ian. Matt could hear the surprise in his mum's voice even from two hundred miles away up the M40.

Ian passed the phone to him.

'Hi, Mum,' he said laconically. 'How's it going?'

His mum explained that the Dachshund Five were going over really well, that she'd made a number of contacts in the dachshund accessories business which she was keen to follow up, that a number of her dogs – Mitch, Tony and Baron von Munchausen – had taken various prizes, and that all in all it was proving to be a very successful season.

'What have you been up to?' she said.

Matt hesitated – should he tell her about his adventures in the world of stand-up comedy or keep it to himself? Something inside him told him not to get her too excited. He also didn't want a big fuss.

'Oh, the usual,' he said. 'School . . . and that.'

'Ian tells me you've been in a bit of trouble with the headmaster.'

'Yes, a bit, but it was nothing much.' He covered the phone with his hand and mouthed a sarcastic 'Thank you' to Ian, who was hanging on his every word.

'Oh, Matt, you promised me you'd be good. Ian's very busy at work . . .'

'That's what he tells you,' thought Matt.

'. . . And the last thing he needs is the school phoning up and hassling him because you've been playing silly beggars.'

'Sorry, Mum,' Matt said reluctantly, looking Ian in the eye.

'It's not me you need to apologise to, it's Ian.'

'Sorry, Ian,' said Matt, rolling his eyes. Ian pulled a similar face back.

'Is there something else going on?' said his mum in a concerned voice.

'Like what?' said Matt.

'Are you being cyber-bullied? I saw a programme

about it. Apparently some children use their computers to bully other children, I'm not quite sure how it works . . .'

'They hit the other kids over the head with them!' said Matt with a grin.

'Children can be so cruel . . .' said his mum, sounding really worried.

'Mum . . . ?' interjected Matt. 'I'm joking, I'm not being cyber-bullied.'

'Look, darling, I'm serious. If you need someone to talk to, Ian's there and I'm back in a week.'

'Yes, Mum.'

'Right then. Can you hand me back to Ian now, please?'

Matt passed the phone to his stepdad.

'Hello again, cutie pie!' he said.

CUTIE PIE

Matt wrote down 'cutie pie' in his little book – then 'How cute can a pie actually look?' and 'Does it work for Cornish pasties too?' Then he gathered up his comedy homework and headed upstairs. He had a routine to write.

24

T Is for Talent

'OK, we need to get some ten-by-eights ...' said Kitty, spreading out some papers on one of the library tables.

'Ten by ... ?'

'Eights – ten inches by eight inches – large-format photographs, publicity shots. We need to get your face out there,' she said, rooting around in her tote bag. 'I also suggest we get along to the venue in advance so you're not completely phased when you turn up on Saturday.'

'Saturday? ... Turn up to the venue ... ? What venue? What are you talking about, Kitty?'

'I've entered you into *The T Factor*!'

As the words tumbled out of her mouth Matt felt like he'd been hit by a ten-ton truck. His head was reeling, he had a ringing noise in his ears, a kind of mist descended in front of his eyes and he thought he was going to have a heart attack right there in the reference section of Anglebrook School Library.

'But . . . but . . .' he stuttered, 'I've only done one gig!'

'Two if you count the talent show. You'll need to sign these,' said Kitty, handing him a bundle of papers with the familiar *T Factor* logo on them. 'Don't worry about that, you may have very little experience at the moment, but over the next five days we're going to get you match fit. You can run through your routines with me in break time. We'll do a couple of workshops nearer the time in front of friends. How are you fixed in the evenings?'

'Um, evenings? Er, fine, but . . .'

'Good. I've had a word with a friend of my dad's – he runs a hotel in Frittledean, the

Cavendish – it's only small, family-run, but they have a function room and he's prepared to take a chance on a sort of junior talent show. Another act in my stable will do the warm-up. It's all here in this itinerary,' she said, handing him a piece of paper with 'Matt Millz Itinerary' printed on it. 'I thought I might have missed the boat with *The T Factor*, but it turns out it's been a quiet year and they're desperate for acts, particularly stand-ups—'

'STOP!' yelled Matt, putting his hands up. Everyone in the library turned to look at him. There was a loud 'Tut!' from the head librarian.

At last Kitty stopped talking and allowed Matt to speak.

'I'm too young, Kitty. I'm only twelve. You have to be sixteen for *The T Factor*.'

'That's a mere detail. Leave it with me.'

'A detail?!' said Matt, glancing down his new itinerary. 'Hang on, you've spelled my name wrong as well! It's Mills with an "s", not a "z".'

'It was, but it isn't now,' said Kitty matter-of-factly.

'You changed my name without asking me?' said Matt incredulously.

'Tweaked it. I just think Matt Millz sounds a bit more showbiz.'

'Ladies and gentlemen, put your hands together for Matt Millz!' said Matt, giving it a road test. 'Hmmm. I could give it a try I suppose.'

'Good, that's what I hoped you'd say, so I took the liberty of . . .'

She reached into her bag and produced a bundle of photocopied A5 flyers emblazoned with the legend 'Kitty Hope Promotions presents *Live at the Cavendish Hotel Junior Showtime* featuring Matt Millz: The Youngest Stand-up Comedian in the World'.

'Wow!' thought Matt. 'This girl's serious.'

'You mentioned another act from your stable doing the warm-up,' he said. 'Who else is in your stable exactly?'

'A dance act, I think you know him.'

A familiar face appeared from around a nearby bookcase and broke into a huge smile.

'Hi, Matt! I'm really looking forward to working with you – again!' It was Neil Trottman.

25

The Workout

The next day at first break, instead of taking up his usual position to shoot the breeze with Rob and Ahmed on the steps outside the science block, Matt met his new manager in the DMC (Disused Mobile Classroom).

'Fame costs, and right here is where you start paying,' said Kitty Hope, sitting backwards on a desk chair with her arms folded, resting on its back.

'Wow! That's a powerful statement, did you make it up yourself?' said Matt, impressed.

'No, I saw it in a film once,' said Kitty.

'How do you know so much about show business, Kitty?' said Matt, taking a seat next to her.

'My grandpa was a big impresario back in the fifties,' she said.

'Impres—?' said Matt quizzically.

'Impresario – like an agent and promoter. Bernie Hopestein. He used to run a number of theatres in the West End.'

'Don't you mean London's *glittering* West End?' said Matt with a chuckle. 'It's never just "the West End", it's always "London's glittering West End!"'

'You're right,' laughed Kitty. 'Sorry, London's glittering West End. Grandpa Bernie booked some of the greatest entertainers who ever lived into the finest theatres ever built. He even booked Laurel and Hardy into the London Palladium!

LAUREL & HARDY

Yes, he was quite something, my grandpa. There's a blue plaque dedicated to him on the wall outside the Apollo.'

'The Apollo?' said Matt. 'The actual Apollo?'

'The actual Apollo,' said Kitty proudly.

'Where they film the TV show?'

'The very same, and incidentally where you're going to be doing your audition for *The T Factor.'*

'No way!' Matt said, a look of utter amazement on his face. 'You're kidding?!! Me at the Apollo?! Wait till I tell Rob!'

'It's going to be really weird for you walking out in front of that many strangers, but remember, they all really want to be entertained and are hoping you're the one who is going to do it for them.'

She picked up a piece of chalk off the floor and started to write on the old blackboard.

Audience Dynamics

1. Audience: All facing the same way — preferably towards the stage!

2. Lights: Keep the audience in the dark, this makes them less self-conscious about laughing and clapping. Bright lights on the stage, focused as much as possible on the comedian.

3. Temperature: People laugh more when they're cooler, less when they're hot — so ventilation's vital.

4. Stage: Ideally raised, with a black curtain behind — the so-called 'Black Box.' As few distractions as possible.

5. Sound: Loud enough so the audience don't have to make any effort to hear – but not so loud that it's feeding back or painful on the ears. Plenty of 'top', not so much 'bass', unlike music – the audience need to understand what you're saying.

6. Chill – out zone or dressing room: This is a luxury in most clubs but ideally you need somewhere to get away from any other distractions and concentrate on your set for the gig.

7. Exits: Ideally there's a back exit so if it goes really badly you don't have to do the walk of shame through the audience to leave the building!

'Grandpa used to say that an audience is like a huge multi-celled organism – although it's made up of individual people from all walks of life, somehow they manage to behave as one. Just like any other organism, various things can affect the way it behaves. Temperature – a hot audience doesn't laugh as much as a cold one. Lighting – an audience in darkness will laugh longer and harder than one brightly lit. Sound – as soon as an audience has to strain to hear what's being offered they become distracted. It's all about making it easy for the crowd to focus on one thing – you! The stand-up comedian at the centre of the stage.'

Matt nodded, totally concentrating on Kitty's speech.

'Very few of them want you to fail, but if they sense the slightest sign of weakness they'll strike as one and gobble you up. An audience needs feeding and your job as a comic is to sling that beast some nice fat juicy jokes to munch on.'

Matt nodded again. What she was saying made a lot of sense. He just couldn't work out how she appeared to know so much at such a young age.

'Now we haven't got time for chit-chat,' she said, sitting down on the backwards chair. 'We need to get down to business. Give me your best five minutes.'

Matt got up, walked ten paces or so and turned to face her. Kitty produced her beloved clipboard and a stopwatch. She nodded to Matt and started the stopwatch running.

Matt took a deep breath. Through the portakabin window he could see Rob and Ahmed across the playground, laughing and joking.

'Hey! Hi, everyone! I'm Matt Millz and I—'

'STOP!' shouted Kitty, banging her clipboard on the back of her chair and clicking the stopwatch.

'Eh?' said Matt, a little flummoxed.

'You don't need to tell us who you are. The MC just did that'

'Oh, right, sorry!' said Matt, shaking his head.

'Continue,' said Kitty and she started the stopwatch again.

'Hey! You know my favourite TV programme? *Tanned Bloke in the Attic . . .*'

'STOP!' yelled Kitty, clicking the stopwatch off again.

'What now?' said Matt. At this rate they were going to be there all day.

'At least say hello!' said Kitty.

'Oh yeah, OK, sorry.' He took another deep breath. Kitty started the stopwatch and off they went again.

'Hi! Great to see you. Thanks! Hey, you know my favourite TV programme? *Tanned Bloke in the Attic* . . .'

'STOP!' Again Kitty slammed down her clipboard. 'Listen, what's the first thing people are going to think when they see you walk on that stage?'

'Um . . . that I'm in the wrong place?' answered Matt. He was starting to wish he'd never clapped eyes on Miss Kitty Hope.

'Exactly!'

'Oh thanks!' said Matt, running his hand through his hair in desperation.

'What I mean is when you walk on, the first thing the audience will see is your age, that you're very young to be a stand-up comedian.'

'Yeah, well I am . . . too young as it happens,' said Matt.

'Yes. So acknowledge it. Refer to it. Better still, make a joke about it. It's the elephant in the room otherwise.'

'The elephant?'

'Yes! A big part of comedy is pointing out the obvious, it's telling the audience in a funny way what they already know but hadn't realised.'

'Example?' said Matt, hands on hips.

'Um . . . OK, take Omid Djalili.'

Omid Djalili Fact File

Style: Great physical routines, uses his size really well. Of Iranian descent, so lots of references to racial stereotypes and attitudes towards the Middle East

Background: Trained as an actor,
still appears in a lot of big
movies (e.g. The Mummy)

Influences: Ivor Dembina, the Two
Ronnies

Top Gag: Geordie woman who woke
up one day with a Jamaican
accent!

Homework: No Agenda: Live at
the London Palladium (2007)

Matt nodded. He was a big fan of the roly-poly
Anglo-Iranian comic.

'When Omid comes on, because he looks like he's
from the Middle East, everyone thinks he's going to
talk in a Middle Eastern accent. So he plays up to it,
even though he's from London. Then when he starts
talking in his normal voice, it's hilarious! A joke

about your appearance is a nice easy gag to make the audience like you.'

'OK, listen, I'm going to have to work on that,' said Matt. He could see the sense in what Kitty was suggesting. 'Leave that with me. Do you want me to carry on or . . . ?'

Kitty nodded vigorously. 'Yes, absolutely, you don't get off that lightly!' she said. 'Run it all past me. These notes are just my ideas. In the end it's up to you. I'm never going to tell you what to say, and if I do, tell me to stop. If I had all the answers I'd be a comedian myself. Right,' she said, holding the stopwatch up for a fourth time. 'Off you go!'

'Hi! Great to see you! Thanks! Hey, you know my favourite TV programme? *Tanned Bloke in the Attic*! You know, the one where you go up into your loft to get something and there's an orange bloke sorting through your stuff so he can flog it to the highest bidder. In fact, talking of antiques, I took my nan along to a recording of *The Antiques Roadshow* the other week – I got two hundred quid for her!'

ORANGE MAN IN THE ATTIC

He looked at Kitty. There wasn't so much as a flicker of a smile on her lips.

'Um, sorry, can we stop a second?' said Matt, feeling rather deflated.

Kitty clicked the stopwatch off and looked up. 'What's up?' she said.

'Am I talking rubbish or ...'

'No, no, I'm really enjoying it,' she said.

'Well, try telling your face!' said Matt. 'You're not laughing.'

'I'm analysing it. I can't laugh at stuff when I'm working.'

'Great, thanks for telling me. It's like doing stand-up to a brick wall! Right, where was I?'

'From the top please, Matt!' said Kitty, jotting something down on her clipboard. And off he went again.

'Hi! Great to see you! Thanks! Hey, you know my favourite TV programme? *Tanned Bloke in the Attic . . .*'

And so it went on for the entire twenty-minute break and then again for an hour over lunch. Matt ran his routine over and over for Kitty and each time she had something to say about it. 'Take longer over the set-up on that one . . . maybe shift that gag earlier . . . make sure you leave a pause for the laughs there.' It was like a trainer working with a boxer for a shot at the world title. If this was a film, thought Matt, he'd be hearing the theme from *Rocky*. By the end of the day his routine had been turned upside down and sideways. Matt didn't know whether he was coming or going, and he was tired – really, really tired.

'Thanks, Matt, we're getting there. Go home tonight, do your DVD homework and sort out those notes, and I'll see you back here tomorrow, first break, to go through it again.'

Matt nodded and headed off towards his afternoon lessons. Double maths would seem like a doddle compared to a session with Kitty Hope.

26

Addicted to Laughs

That evening a photo of a genial-looking gent shaking hands with a young Queen Elizabeth II loaded up on to Matt's laptop. It was on the Wikipedia page for Sir Bernie Hopestein – Kitty's illustrious showbiz ancestor.

> <u>Sir Bernie Hopestein Fact File</u>
>
> Born: 1928
>
> Background: Trained as a dancer, then became an agent, promoter and theatre owner. Managing Director Hopestein Associates Ltd.

Ran the Finsbury Park Empire,
the Hackney Empire, the Chiswick
Empire, the London Palladium
and Hammersmith Odeon (later
renamed the Apollo)

Acts: Bob Hope, Frank Sinatra,
Elvis Presley, the Beatles, Tommy
Cooper, Jimmy Tarbuck, Judy
Garland, Laurel and Hardy,
Morecambe and Wise, the
Two Ronnies

Knighted by HM the Queen
in 1969

Catchphrase: Do it again, only
this time bigger!

The photo had been taken at the Royal Variety Show at the London Palladium way back in 1962. Reading through the entry Matt was impressed. This guy had virtually run show business during the latter part of the last century. There were photographs of him with Bob Hope, Frank Sinatra, Elvis Presley, the Beatles, Tommy Cooper, Jimmy Tarbuck, Judy Garland, Laurel and Hardy, the Two Ronnies – the list went on. It seemed his granddaughter Kitty was stepping into very big shoes indeed.

Matt turned to his little black book, scanning it for his best gags: *My mother was a lollipop lady: she had a long thin body and a big round sticky head* … Hmmm, not bad … *Acupuncture's good for a lot of medical problems, but not for pins and needles – because that's what it is!* … Nice … *I like Chimpanzees but why do they always go for that middle parting?'*

He was still looking for a gag about his appearance to open his set with. 'I know a lot of you are looking at me thinking – good heavens, he's young! It's true, I'm so young that if I'm having a drink I still like to have a rusk with it. Sure, I've got skinny legs, but the upside is I can still get them through the leg holes in a shopping trolley so I get a free ride round ASDA – and in that position I'm just the right height for the Hobnobs!'

That sounded pretty funny to Matt as he was saying it. Hobnobs were a good comedy standby – they must have appeared in more routines than any other biscuit. But he'd learnt over the past few weeks that there was a big difference between what one person found funny and what made a whole room of strangers laugh.

Every day that week followed the same pattern. At first break, every lunch break and after school Matt would report to the DMC. Together he and Kitty would work on his routine, honing it, polishing it, getting it to time. Then, when Matt got home, he'd wolf down one of Ian's cooked-from-frozen dinners and race upstairs to practise in front of the mirror, hairbrush in hand.

Matt had decided against telling Ian about *The T Factor*. He didn't want him to make a fuss, and thought he might disapprove of his hoodwinking the judges about his age. In fact, he and Kitty agreed that they shouldn't tell anyone – not even Rob. 'The fewer people who know about it, the less likely your secret is to get out,' she said.

'Everything all right, Matt?' said Ian one evening as they sat on the sofa waiting for their dinner to cook. It was one of Mum's chicken pies. They'd been getting on a lot better since their bonding session in front of Kitty's Classic Comedy DVD collection – in fact it had become a regular fixture of their evenings together. 'It's just that I've hardly seen you these last few days. I wondered if you fancied watching this?' He reached under the coffee table and produced a DVD. 'It's that Stewart Lee bloke you were talking about the other day.'

Stewart Lee Fact File

Style: Deadpan, takes an anti-populist stance. Berates the audience for not being clever enough to understand his gags

Background: Birmingham-born. Got his first break as part of double act Lee and Herring in 1990s

Influences: Ted Chippington, Simon Munnery, Kevin McAleer

Top gag: 'I found this place that does really good Italian food — it's Italy.'

Homework: Stewart Lee's Comedy Vehicle, BBC TV 2009-16

Even though Matt was a fan of the wonderfully sarcastic, tubby Midlands comic, he shook his head. 'Not tonight I'm afraid, Ian. I've got work to do.'

A look of concern settled on Ian's face. He carefully placed the DVD on the coffee table and stood up. He paced up and down awkwardly, adjusting various ornaments as he went, and then he turned to Matt. He looked like he had the weight of the world on his shoulders.

'Matt, you would tell me if you were on drugs, wouldn't you?' said Ian, putting a hand on his shoulder.

Matt couldn't help himself, he started laughing. 'Drugs! Ha ha! Wherever did you get that idea?!' he giggled.

'Well, I read a thing about how to tell your child is on drugs – it said they become suddenly secretive, you hardly see them, they seem preoccupied with something – that's *you*!'

'I've got a big gig, Ian. That's all I can tell you at this stage. It might just be my big break.'

'Thank heavens!' said Ian, looking relieved. 'I've been worried sick at how I was going to break it to your mum!'

'Yes, you've got nothing to worry about on that score. The only drug I'm into is laughter!'

'Phew!' said Ian. 'It's just that I've seen the damage drugs can do.'

'You have?' said Matt, sitting up. 'When?'

'You know, when I was dabbling in the fringes of punk rock – the band I was telling you about.'

'Right,' said Matt, turning uncharacteristically serious.

'And on that score,' continued Ian, 'I popped back to my mum's house yesterday and had a root around some of my old stuff and I found this!'

Ian got up and retrieved a carrier bag from the kitchen table. He reached into it and pulled out a battered old scrapbook.

'Wow!' said Matt, taking the scrapbook and flicking through the pages of faded photos, printed leaflets and press cuttings. His eye was caught by a black-and-white photo of some spotty youths in leather jackets and tartan trousers leering at the camera.

'Who the heck are they?'

'That, Matt, is the original line-up of Dead Toys – Bromley's foremost undiscovered punk rock band!'

'No way! You're joking!' said Matt. 'So, hang on, that means that weirdo on the drums with the mohican . . . no . . . it can't be! That's you?!'

''Fraid so!' Ian nodded, joining Matt on the sofa. 'Pretty cool, even if I do say so myself! That photo was taken only a few days after I'd pierced my nose with a safety pin – that's why it's all swollen. I got an infection on the day of the photo and had to go on antibiotics.'

'Not so cool,' said Matt, laughing. He couldn't believe that the middle-aged bloke sitting next to him had once been a young man with dreams – just like him.

'Yeah. While I was round my mum's I got the old drum kit out too – stuck it in the car. Mum couldn't wait to see the back of them, to be honest. That's the problem with being a drummer – your instrument is massive.'

'Give us a tune then.'

'Well I wasn't planning to *play* them, I was going to see what I could get for them on eBay.'

'You should set them up and have a play! Go on, go and get them!'

'Well, if you think . . . Maybe I will, just for old time's sake.'

There was a 'Ping!' as the microwave finished its important work and Matt sifted through the rest of the scrapbook as Ian served up their dinner.

'You certainly are a dark horse, Ian, I never would have guessed it. Oh, and by the way, I think this might need a bit longer in the microwave,' laughed Matt, tapping the rock-hard frozen chicken pie. 'Unless you're planning to serve it with wafers!'

27

Friends Reunited

'You coming down Greggs?' said Rob the next day in first break. It was the first time he'd seen him to talk to in days.

'Um, sorry, Rob,' said Matt sheepishly, 'I've got to see Kitty.'

'Oh yeah, I forgot, your new girlfriend,' said Rob sniffily.

'Er, she's my manager?' said Matt.

'Hm! Well, that's fine, but don't forget we've got a "Pavey's Punchlines" to do.'

'Oh yeah, totally forgot. Sorry, Rob. I've got this gig at the Cavendish in Frittledean on Friday so I've got my head down working on that. It's not great either, because as of this morning they hadn't shifted any tickets. I don't s'pose you could do "Pavey's Punchlines" on your own this week?'

'Um, like no?' said Rob, screwing up his face.

'OK, leave it with me, I'll see you at lunch break – no, wait, I'm seeing Kitty again then. Look, I'll text you, yeah?'

'Whatever!' said Rob, heading off towards Ahmed and a couple of the others up by the steps outside the science block.

Matt knew he'd become a rather distant figure and if he was honest, he missed Rob like hell. They'd had a routine together – not a comedy one but a social one – meet up before school at the gates for a chat, meet first break outside the science block for banter, or if they had any cash they'd head down Greggs in the town, then it was school dinner and general horsing around with Ahmed and the guys. With Rob there was always some new adventure or plan hatching.

Although he knew Rob wasn't cut out for a career in comedy – or personal management – Matt still wanted him to be involved with his success, or, as they said on *The T Factor*, his *journey*. But how?

On the day before the gig at the Cavendish Hotel, Kitty invited a few friends to the DMC to watch Matt do his set during lunch break. Matt had asked a few of his pals too – principally Rob and Ahmed. It had gone pretty well. It had certainly shown them both where the holes in the routine were and what needed to be improved but mainly it was a huge relief for Matt to hear genuine laughter.

'That was sweeeeeet, bruv!' said Ahmed, high-fiving Matt moments after he'd finished. 'Love the stuff about you looking so young, because, like, you do! Ha ha!'

'Cheers for coming, Ahmed,' said Matt. 'Rob not able to make it?'

'Ah, Mr Brown, no, he didn't manage to make his

way over to the Disused Mobile Classroom Theatre.'

'Oh, that's a shame, I'd wanted to see what he thought.'

'Truth is, bruv, your friend Rob has got the hump with you.'

'I guessed as much.'

'He misses you, man. You don't hang around with us any more.'

'Yeah, but it's only for this week!' said Matt.

'Well, don't tell me, tell him.' Ahmed gestured towards the main school.

'Yeah, Ahmed, you're right. I will.'

Matt skipped down the corridor towards his first lesson of the afternoon and saw Rob standing by the lockers, chatting to Magda Avery.

'Hey, Rob, Magda!' said Matt.

'Hello, stranger!' said Rob drily.

'Rob! You didn't fancy coming to the little gig I just did then?' said Matt.

'Sorry, mate, couldn't make it, I've been working on my own little project,' said Rob.

'All right, Magda?' said Matt.

'Yeah, Rob tells me you're going to be a big star,' said Magda. 'He says you ain't got time for your old friends no more.'

'Magda!' hissed Rob.

'Well, you did say that, so . . .' she tailed off. 'Oh please yourself. See you round my place later.' She sauntered off down the corridor without so much as a glance at Matt.

'Round her place?' exclaimed Matt as they both watched her disappear. 'You and her seem to be getting on very well.'

'Yeah, it's this portrait. It's proving quite tricky – she just won't sit still! It's needing lots of sessions. I think she's enjoying the attention, to be honest.'

'Well, just watch out for Dave Joy's fists – remember Ahmed's nose.'

'Ah, if it isn't Mills and Brown! I was a little disappointed to see no "Pavey's Punchlines" this week in the school mag.' It was Mr Gillingham. 'What's up? Run out of ideas?'

Matt bristled at the very suggestion that his creative well had dried up.

'No, we didn't have time this week,' he replied.

'HE didn't have time, he means,' said Rob.

'Oh dear, do I detect a rift in the creative team? Artistic differences starting to surface?'

The two boys shifted uneasily, neither volunteering an answer.

'Listen, you two, I wouldn't say this to just anyone, but I love that page you do for the magazine. It's sharp, it's funny – you work really well together. So next week I want to see it back, is that understood?'

'OK,' they both said together.

'Good. Sort out your problems and get on with it.'

Mr G headed off towards the staff room. An awkward silence ensued. The two boys stood staring into space, trying to avoid each other's gaze. It was Matt who broke the stalemate.

'Perhaps we should go on Jeremy Kyle,' he said.

'Yeah, and the title of the show would be "I Lost My Friend to Comedy".'

'Sorry about this week, Rob.'

'Well, you're never around *ever*, Matt!' said Rob. 'We used to hang out all the time – round the science block, mucking about down the town – the joke page ... Greggs – there's sausage rolls left uneaten that we could be munching on!'

'Oh, so it's the sausage rolls you're missing mainly, is it?'

'You know what I mean,' said Rob.

'Yeah, I know. I've just been really busy with this stand-up thing.'

'You've got a gig at the Cavendish Hotel in Frittledean – it's not exactly the Apollo, is it?'

'But that's just it!' began Matt, then checked himself. 'Um ...'

'What?' said Rob suspiciously.

'Nothing. Um ... it's only the Cavendish Hotel in Frittledean to you, but you know what they say? If you can make it in Frittledean, you can make it anywhere!'

'Ha!' said Rob, loosening up. 'Frittledean – the city that ALWAYS sleeps!'

'Good one!' said Matt, reaching for his little black book. 'I'll have that.'

'Ahem! Have you seen the time, Matt?' It was Kitty.

'Blimey, where did you spring from?' said Matt. Because of her height she had a habit of sneaking up on people unannounced.

'You haven't forgotten, have you? We've got our little trip,' she said.

'Trip?' said Rob with a raised eyebrow.

'Yes, Rob, we have a trip to London – I mean Frittledean – planned,' said Kitty, quickly correcting herself. Lying really wasn't in her nature, which might prove a bit of a stumbling block in her future career.

'Great, I've heard the nightlife is to die for,' said Rob.

'Of course, yeah, no, I hadn't forgotten,' said Matt. 'Sorry, Rob, I'm going to have to dash. Look, it's a bit of a busy week for me. Can we meet up next week instead?'

'How are tickets shifting?' said Rob, looking at Kitty.

'We're expecting a lot of sales on the door,' said Kitty defensively.

'How many?' persisted Rob.

'Four,' said Matt with an embarrassed smile, '... and those have been bought by Neil Trottman's mum and dad.'

'He's right,' said Kitty. 'It's not looking good. What we need is some way of getting word out there that it's happening.'

'What, you mean like a poster?' said Rob, a grin spreading across his face.

'A poster would be great. I had a few flyers printed but they looked a bit rubbish. They were supposed to do some publicity at the Cavendish but I'm afraid I didn't chase them about it. Sorry, Matt.'

'A poster, a bit like ...' Rob reached into his sports bag, produced a piece of rolled-up paper and unfurled it with a flourish. 'Ta-da! ... This!' It was a full-colour caricature of Matt in his stage outfit, holding a microphone with 'Comedy Night. Matt Millz Live from the Cavendish!' emblazoned across it.

'Wow!' said Matt and Kitty in unison.

'That's brilliant!' said Kitty.

'It must have taken ages!' said Matt.

'Glad you like it. It took me a little while – that's why I couldn't get to your lunchtime try-out.'

'After this you can have as many free tickets for tomorrow night as you want!' said Kitty. 'This is going to give sales just the boost they need. Thanks, Rob! You're a wonder!' she said and gave him a big hug.

'I can nip into the library after school and print off some copies on the school magazine account,' said Rob, carefully rolling the poster up.

For once Matt Mills was speechless. 'I don't know what to say,' he said eventually. 'All that time I thought you were fed up, in fact you were working to help me. Thanks, Rob,' and he too gave his old friend a hug.

'Sorry to break up the party but we've got a train to catch,' interjected Kitty.

'Oh right, yeah,' said Matt. He looked apologetically at Rob.

'Don't worry, you go. I'll get these posters printed.'

'Cheers, Rob,' said Matt, and he and Kitty walked briskly towards the school gates.

'Can't I even tell Rob about the audition, Kit?' said Matt once they were safely out of school.

'No, we discussed this, remember? The fewer people who know about the *T Factor* audition the better.'

'Oh come on, Kitty. Just Rob . . . please?' pleaded Matt.

'Look, I can't stop you, but as your manager I can advise you that that's a really bad idea.'

'All right, I'll think about it.'

He did think about it and it took only a moment to come to the conclusion that Kitty had been proved right so far and that really he ought to take her advice. He wouldn't tell Rob – despite longing to see the look on his face when he finally did.

28

One Giant Leap

It was early evening by the time they got to the Hammersmith Apollo. Kitty's mum had picked them both up from school and dropped them at Staplefirst station in time for them to get the train up to Charing Cross. Then they'd taken a tube across London to Hammersmith and from there it was a relatively short walk.

'I'll do the talking,' said Kitty, marching up the front steps. She pushed open the huge polished brass-handled doors and they walked inside. The foyer was a riot of gold, glass and red velvet. Up above them a crystal chandelier glittered and gleamed, scattering light that illuminated framed posters of every stand-up comedian who had ever graced that hallowed stage.

Matt could feel a lump coming to his throat. 'Wow! We're really here!'

'Yup!' said Kitty with a broad grin, proud that her little plan had so far gone without a hitch.

'Look! There's a poster of Eddie!' He was pointing at a big glossy poster of his hero Eddie Odillo, sat with arms outstretched on the back of a Shetland pony.

'Yes, he sold out fourteen nights here.'

'Fourteen nights! No wonder, that's a great poster!' said Matt.

'You're right,' agreed Kitty. 'It's cool but it's also funny, it tells you something about Eddie's style of humour. He's not afraid to look silly either. Grandpa Bernie used to say there's no room for vanity in comedy – that's for all the other wings of showbiz!'

'Yes? Can I help you?' said an officious-looking old gent in a red tailcoat and peaked cap.

'Wilfred Bramble?' said Kitty, thrusting her calling card into his gloved hand. 'Kitty Hope, I'm here with Matt Millz, stand-up comedian. I'm sure Giles told you we'd be coming?'

'Oh, er . . . not that I can remember . . .'

'Matt's on at the weekend and just wanted to run through his technical requirements with Ken. All right if we go on in? We'll only be ten minutes.'

Her confident approach took old Wilfred by surprise. Stopping Kitty Hope when she was in full flow was like trying to stop a rhinoceros with a leaf blower.

'Well, if Giles okayed it then I . . .'

'Thank you, Wilfred. How's Mrs B?'

'Oh! A lot better, thank you, still walks with a slight limp but . . .'

Before he had time to finish his story they'd gone. They swished through the next set of swing doors and into the auditorium.

'How did you know his name and who's Giles?' asked Matt, struggling to keep up with her as she marched up through the rows of seats.

'Google,' said Kitty, pulling out her smartphone and taking a couple of photos.

'Ah yes, of course,' said Matt. 'But how did you know he was married?'

'He's wearing a wedding ring, bit of a gamble I admit, but it paid off.'

'Sherlock Holmes eat your heart out, eh?'

'Confidence is everything, Matt. You should remember that when you're on that stage on Saturday. Grandpa always said that stand-up comedians are glorified door-to-door salesmen, only the product they're selling is jokes! An audience will buy even a not-great joke, if you sell it and look like you mean it.'

'And their payment is a laugh?'

'Exactly! Some comics are funny people saying not particularly funny things, others are not particularly funny people saying very funny things. If you've got both, you could be great – provided you have the third thing.'

'Staying power?'

'You're learning!'

For the next few minutes Matt looked like something out of a cartoon. His eyes were on stalks and his tongue lolled out of his mouth as he stared from the back of the theatre up at the stage. That stage where every great singer, dancer, magician and of course comedian who ever topped a bill had played. He could see exactly the spot where Eddie Odillo stood every Friday night for ten weeks doling out the laughs in his *Stand-up at the Apollo* TV show.

Kitty walked up to the front of the stalls and

beckoned to him. By the time he got there she was standing centre stage.

'Come on up!' she said, waving him on.

And Matt made those eight steps that are the difference between being a member of the audience and being a performer.

'One small step for a man but a giant leap for me!' said Matt, as he walked over to join Kitty. He looked out over the hundreds of empty seats.

'Three thousand six hundred and thirty-two, in case you're wondering,' said Kitty, looking right up to the top tier or upper circle, known as 'the gods'.

<u>Theatre terms</u>

Backstage: Areas of the theatre next to the stage accessible only to performers and technicians, including the wings and dressing rooms.

Proscenium arch: The arch framing the stage.

Wings: Areas left and right just behind the proscenium arch, used for performers waiting to go on, for storage of parts of sets and props, and for technical equipment like the sound desk. The wings are masked from the audience's view using long hanging curtains or 'legs'.

Apron: The area of the stage in front of the proscenium arch.

Crossover: The area used by performers and technicians to travel from stage left to right unseen by the audience, usually screened off with a curtain.

Prompt corner: The area just to one side of the proscenium arch where the stage manager stands to cue the show.

Rake: The downward slope in the stage that gives the audience a better view.

Safety curtain: A heavy fireproof curtain just behind the proscenium arch which can be lowered to contain any potential fire. Often referred to as 'the iron', as that's what they used to be made of.

Orchestra pit: The deep trench in front of the stage where the orchestra sit and play.

Auditorium: The section of the theatre where the audience sits. From the ground up it goes Stalls, Dress Circle (and Boxes) and finally the Upper Circle ('the gods').

'Three thousand six hundred and thirty-two what?' said Matt.

'Seats,' said Kitty.

'Holy moly!' said Matt.

'For God's sake put that tongue away before a fly lands on it and lays an egg!' said Kitty. 'Yes, it's a big place, but when it's full – imagine the laughs!'

Matt didn't need to. He'd heard them every Saturday night through his TV as Eddie Odillo and his other heroes did their routines. He pushed his tongue back into his mouth with his finger.

'That's funny!' said Kitty with a laugh.

'What is?' said Matt, confused.

'Pushing your tongue in like that, like a cartoon – you should keep that in.'

'Won't it make me look kind of dumb?'

'No, you'll be telling the audience exactly what they're thinking. That you look a bit young and inexperienced to be on this stage. Remember, it's the elephant in the room, so best to acknowledge it – and get a laugh out of it.'

'Hmmm, that's something I can work on.'

'Hey! What do you think you're playing at?!' a gruff voice bellowed from the back of the stalls.

'Uh-oh, looks like I just got my first heckle!' whispered Matt.

'Giles?' said Kitty, stepping down off the stage and heading to where the voice was coming from. As they got halfway they saw Wilfred flapping his arms around like a parrot on heat, and standing next to him a large sweaty man wearing a moustache, a tight-fitting pinstriped suit – and a frown. He did not look very happy at all.

'No. Not Giles. Try again, madam!' he said.

'Sorry, Mr Purbright,' said Wilfred, 'they just barged in! She said that Giles had okayed it!'

'There's been a mistake, we were due at the Palladium! No harm done,' said Kitty, dragging Matt behind her and heading for the swing doors.

'Wait!' said Mr Purbright, putting an arm out and barring their way. 'Not so fast. Do your parents know you're out, Miss Kitty Hope?' he said, reading her name off the card she'd given Wilfred.

'How's Mrs Purbright?!' chirped Matt.

'Died three years ago!' said Mr Purbright. His tone had changed from gruff to angry now.

'Ooops!' thought Matt. It seemed some people still wore a wedding ring even when their partner had snuffed it.

'Shame! Better luck next time!' said Matt cheerfully.

Judging by the look on Mr Purbright's face, that hadn't gone down too well either.

Kitty Hope and Matt Mills's exit from the

Hammersmith Apollo was somewhat less grand than their entrance.

'And stay out!' barked Wilfred and Mr Purbright simultaneously as they gave Matt a final shove out of the Apollo's doors. Matt tripped and rolled knee over elbow down the red-carpeted steps and landed at Kitty's feet.

'Hmm,' he said, looking up at her from the pavement. 'You've got a bogey up your nose!'

Somewhere high up above him there was a squawk and a splodge of white pigeon muck landed on his forehead.

'Welcome to another edition of *Springwatch*!' he quipped, sitting up.

'Serves you right!' laughed Kitty, pulling out a small packet of wet wipes and handing them to Matt.

'Let's hope it goes better than that on Saturday!' he said, rolling his eyes.

Then as he straightened himself up he saw it, about twenty feet above them on the wall of the Apollo – a blue ceramic plaque with white writing on it. 'There it is, Kitty, look!' He pointed at it and read the legend out loud: "Sir Bernie Hopestein, Theatrical Impresario. Managing Director of the Hammersmith Odeon" – that's your grandfather!'

'So it is!' said Kitty. Matt quickly whipped out his smartphone and took a selfie of the two of them with the plaque in the background. Then they scrambled off towards the tube.

Matt got home at about nine, just as it was starting to get dark. As he walked up the front path to the house he thought he could hear a weird banging noise coming from upstairs, like someone was breaking a door down with an iron bar.

'Jeez! We're being burgled!' he thought. He peered through the letterbox. There didn't appear to be any sign of a disturbance.

Suddenly he heard a blood-curdling cry – it was Ian and he was clearly in pain! 'It's worse than I thought! They've taken Ian hostage. They're torturing him!' Without any further thought for his own safety he opened the front door and ran up the stairs. As he got to the landing and turned the corner the banging noise and Ian's cries of agony became ear-splittingly loud. They seemed to be coming from the spare room. Matt was frightened now. What should he do? Press on or phone the police?

He took out his phone but as he was about to dial 999 the door to the spare room started to swing slowly open. Matt peered through the crack. There in front of him, wearing only boxer shorts and headphones, was the sweaty figure of Ian bashing away at a huge drum kit. The headphones were connected to an old-fashioned cassette tape player. The wailing noise was Ian's idea of singing! He had his eyes closed and hadn't noticed Matt coming in.

Matt crept over and flicked the cassette player off at the plug socket. Ian opened his eyes and seeing Matt, let out a yelp. 'Aargh! You scared the life out of me!' he said.

'Likewise,' retorted Matt. 'You got the drums out, then!'

'Yeah!' said Ian. 'I forgot how much fun it was!' He had a twinkle in his eye and an energy about him that Matt hadn't seen in him since the Dachshund Five had won first prize in the musical category at the Berlin dog show.

Matt shook his head in disbelief. 'I was just about to call the police, I thought we were being burgled!'

'Yes, well, I admit I'm a little rusty . . .' said Ian.

'Good job I didn't. They could have arrested you for crimes against music!' laughed Matt.

'Steady! It may sound a bit a ropey but I'm really enjoying it!' said Ian. 'Where have you been, anyway?'

'Rehearsing,' said Matt.

'Well I'm afraid your dinner's stone cold,' said Ian.

'No change there then!' said Matt.

A little later Matt lay on his bed contemplating the

day's events. It was all pretty unbelievable.

He started going through the material he planned to do at the gig tomorrow night at the Cavendish that would hopefully become his *T Factor* set list.

His phone vibrated into life. It was Kitty. 'Hi, Matt, I'm just checking that you're all set for tomorrow?'

'Hi, Kitty. I think I'm OK, I mean I know what I'm planning to do . . . but my main worry is they'll take one look at me and think I'm too young to be a stand-up,' said Matt.

'Yes I know, and it's really important you look older – especially for *The T Factor*, which is why I've got a plan for that,' said Kitty cryptically.

'A plan? What plan?' said Matt.

'Meet me at the DMC after school tomorrow and all will be revealed. You should be feeling good about tomorrow, you've worked really hard this week.'

'Thanks. I've just got to get on with it now. I think I'm funny, you think I'm funny . . . so the chances are, I'm probably funny. So relax. I'll be fine – hey, I feel funny!'

It was true, he thought as he hung up, he did feel funny – but not funny ha-ha, funny peculiar.

Matt selected the selfie he'd taken of the two of them outside the Apollo and forwarded it to Kitty with the caption 'The past – and the future in one photo!'

He was asleep in the time it took for his head to hit the pillow.

29

The DMC Salon

When he got to the DMC Kitty was waiting for him. Next to her was a full-length mirror and a length of material hung up to form a makeshift curtain.

'What's going on, Kitty?' asked Matt suspiciously.

'We need to sort out your look, Matt, so this morning I've invited in a couple of experts.'

'Hello, darlin'!' A large woman of about thirty-five popped her head round the curtain and broke out into a broad grin. 'I understand you liked what I did for my Neil!'

The curtain opened a little further and standing next to her was Neil Trottman.

'Hi, Matt! It wasn't my idea,' he said, with a half-hearted wave.

'No, it was mine,' said Kitty. 'Mrs T has very kindly agreed to fit you up with a new suit.'

From behind the curtain Mrs Trottman wheeled out a rail on which hung an array of suits of all different colours and sizes.

'Neil's auntie has a stall in the market so she gets some nice discount,' said Mrs Trottman. 'Come here, son, let's get you kitted out.'

They spent the next hour trying out different combinations of suits, jackets and trousers. Matt and Kitty eventually agreed on a sharp electric-blue suit that wasn't a million miles away from one he'd seen Eddie Odillo wear on his live stand-up DVD. Mrs T expertly turned up the trousers and took them in so it was more or less an exact fit. As Matt looked at himself in the full-length mirror he felt like a million dollars.

'Thanks, Mrs Trottman!' he said.

'I told ya, call me Angela!' she said with a smile.

'Right, Neil, help me load the rest of this stuff back into the van.'

After they'd gone Matt turned to Kitty, who was looking at her watch.

'You know, I feel a lot more confident in this suit but I still look too young.'

'I know. That brings me to the second part of the plan. I've got someone coming to give you a makeover!' said Kitty, barely able to contain her excitement.

'A makeover!' said Matt, standing back in amazement. 'Who . . . ?'

At that moment the door burst open and in walked Magda Avery, dragging a small suitcase on wheels behind her.

'Hi, Kitty, sorry I'm late. Dave's motorbike broke down half a mile from school. I tell you, that contraption is a right pain! Actually that's probably the last trip I'll be taking on it. Anyway, I'm here now, that's the main thing. Where do you want me?'

'Don't worry, Magda, I'm just really glad you could make it. Matt, this is Magda Avery—'

'I know who this is!' said Matt. 'But what are you doing here, Magda?'

'It seems Magda is a bit of a make-up expert,' continued Kitty. 'She's going to make you look a little older.'

'You know I'm into make-up!' she squealed. 'Now come on, Benjamin Button, let's have a look at you!'

Magda unzipped her suitcase to reveal brushes, combs, hairdryers, all manner of gels and sprays and – rather worryingly for Matt – wigs.

'My mum let me borrow some stuff from the salon. Take a seat, Matt,' she said, pulling up a chair, 'and let's get you sorted.'

Matt sat down warily.

'I love *The T Factor*,' swooned Magda, as she started combing Matt's hair.

'You told her about the gig!?' said Matt, looking accusingly at Kitty.

'I had to, Matt.'

'Oh don't worry about that, I can keep a secret,' said Magda, selecting a long black wavy wig from her suitcase. 'Simon's my favourite judge – the strong silent type. Mind you, I wish I had Amanda's money, although I'm not sure I'd spend it at the same places she does. You see some of the get-ups she was in last year? Half the time she looked like she'd been dragged through a hedge backwards.'

She put the last finishing touches to the wig, gave it a couple of bursts of hairspray and stepped back. 'How about that?'

Matt turned and looked at himself in the mirror. He now had black wavy hair sticking out from his head, and lots of it.

'I look like Russell Brand after he's been strapped to the front of a jumbo jet and flown halfway round the world!' exclaimed Matt.

'No?' said Magda without the slightest trace of disappointment. 'No problem, we've got lots to choose from.'

She dipped back into the suitcase and took out a blond curly wig. She gave it a shake and stretched it on to Matt's head.

'Whoa! Now I look like Taylor Swift after she's wrestled Russell Brand on the front of a jumbo jet that's flown halfway round the world!' he cried, whipping the wig off and tossing it back into the suitcase.

'No?' said Magda. 'No worries, plenty of time, let's try something else.'

This time she tried a wig made of tight ginger curls. Matt started laughing.

'Hi, my name's Ed Sheeran, hello, Wembley!' he joked. 'This is crazy!'

'Well, it's getting the right reaction,' said Magda. 'You're laughing, aintcha?'

'They're the wrong sort of laughs!'

'OK, let's start again. In my book on stage make-up it says a little bit of talcum powder put on the hair can give it a grey effect,' she said, shaking a tub of talc over Matt's hair. Unfortunately, whoever had used it last hadn't put the lid on properly and the entire contents landed in a pile on top of Matt's head and cascaded down his face.

'Merry Christmas, everybody!' chortled Matt.

'Whoops!' said Magda.

'I look like a corpse with a dandruff problem,' laughed Matt.

'How about a pipe or a bit of facial hair?' said Magda, brushing the talc off as best she could and ramming a pipe into Matt's mouth. She then peeled the backing off a self-adhesive moustache and plonked it on to Matt's top lip.

'Now I look like Ahmed's dad!' cried Matt. 'Tell her to stop, Kitty!'

'Ahem!' said Kitty, approaching Magda cautiously. 'I think we need to go a bit more ... well ... subtle, Magda. It's probably more about a slightly more mature hairstyle than wigs as such. It needs to look natural.'

'Well why didn't you say so?' said Magda, rolling her eyes. 'I thought it was for a comedy sketch! I can do natural no problem!'

She delved into her bag, retrieved a tub of some sort of gel and started to apply it to Matt's hair. Then she grabbed a pair of scissors.

'Whoa, what are you going to do with with those?' said Matt.

'Look, Matt, my mum's got her own salon, OK?'

'So?' said Matt.

'So you're just going to have to trust me,' she said, flourishing a comb. Matt looked at Kitty, Kitty nodded and Magda got to work.

Thirty-five minutes later Matt emerged from the DMC Salon and Makeover Centre with a new look. Magda had cut his hair short at the sides and slicked his fringe back over his crown. He had to admit he looked pretty cool and possibly now might even pass for sixteen.

'Not bad,' said Magda as she and Kitty watched Matt make his way across the playground. 'He's quite fanciable! But it's his mate I prefer.'

Kitty rolled her eyes and called after Matt. 'See you at the Cavendish at half past seven!'

Matt turned. 'You betcha!' he shouted. Then under his breath he whispered, 'Let's *do* this thing!'

30
It's Up to You, Frittledean!

The next day Matt woke up raring to go. He'd spent the week honing his act and the 'workshops' in front of friends had gone pretty well, most of the time. In short, he felt match fit and couldn't wait to try out his set, his suit and his haircut in front of a paying audience. He felt he'd learnt more about stand-up comedy in the last week than he had in all the years leading up to it.

His only real difficulty now was getting to the gig. Frittledean was completely off the beaten track. 'The last form of public transport to travel to Frittledean had stone wheels and was pulled by a woolly mammoth,' he joked. 'It makes Biddleden look like Piccadilly Circus!'

'There's nothing for it,' he said to Neil Trottman as they stood at the bus stop at the end of a particularly long day. 'We'll have to hitch-hike.'

'We'll have to what?' said Neil, looking confused.

'Hitch-hike. We stand by the side of the road and stick out our thumbs, and hopefully somebody will stop and give us a lift.'

'I'm not sure my mum would like me doing that,' said Neil. 'I'm only ten!'

'Well, we've got no choice,' said Matt.

'You have got a choice actually,' came a voice from behind them. They turned to see the man-mountain that was Mr Gillingham. He was dangling his car keys in front of them.

'Frittledean, right?' he said.

'Erm, yes!' said Matt. 'How did you ... ?'

'I live there,' said Mr G. 'The village is plastered with Rob's posters for "A Comedy Night" starring "Matt Millz" and "Winner of 'Anglebrook's Got

Talent' Neil Trottman, plus special guests". I'm assuming Toxic Cabbage aren't on the bill?'

'No, sir!' piped up Neil. 'I think the hotel manager's wife is going to sing a couple of songs.'

'Sounds like quite a night,' said Mr Gillingham with a smile. 'You'd better hop in.'

They followed him to his battered old Volkswagen Beetle and climbed aboard.

'Right then,' said Mr G, settling his huge frame into the driver's seat. 'Frittledean or bust!'

He turned the key in the ignition. Nothing. He tried again. No sound was forthcoming – the engine was as quiet as the toilet on a hospital constipation ward.

'Bust then,' deadpanned Matt.

'OK, gents,' said Mr Gillingham, completely unperturbed. 'Out you get, and start pushing!'

Once they'd managed to jumpstart the car, the trip to Frittledean had passed without incident apart from having to put up with Mr Gillingham's singing.

'Blimey, you make Magda Avery sound good, sir!' said Neil.

'Now, now, Neil, she was trying her best – as am I! You're very quiet, Matt, everything all right?'

Mr Gillingham was right. Matt was concentrating on his set list for the gig.

'Yes, sir, just a bit nervous, that's all.'

It wasn't long before they were pulling up the drive to the Cavendish Hotel. Matt could see the diminutive figure of Kitty Hope directing a big man in a suit up a stepladder as he tried to hang a large PVC banner printed with the words 'Comedy Nite'.

'Up a bit your end, Barry, please! No! Too far, down a bit!'

'How's it going, Kitty?' said Matt.

'Wow! You look great!' said Kitty, admiring his new threads.

'Oh, you know this slave driver, do you?' said the bloke up the ladder.

'Er . . . well, she's . . .' stuttered Matt.

'If I appear bossy it's because it needs to be just

right, Barry!' said Kitty sternly. She turned to Matt. 'There's good news and bad news, I'm afraid. Which do you want first?'

'Um, the good news, I guess.'

'The good news is we've sold half the tickets.'

'Half? So that's . . . ?'

'Sixty-eight – which is a perfectly good crowd for a room this size.'

'And the bad news?'

'The bad news is half of them haven't turned up.'

'You've still got forty minutes till show time,' said Barry, climbing down from the ladder and shaking Matt's hand. 'Barry Wonsall, hotel manager. I'm guessing you're the comedian I've heard so much about?'

'That's right. I don't know what Kitty's been saying, but I'm Matt Millz and yes, I'm hoping to be—'

'Not hoping!' barked Kitty. 'You are one – say it!'

'I am a stand-up comedian!' said Matt rather sheepishly.

'According to Kitty here you're the best thing since sliced bread. Who's your friend?' he said, indicating Neil.

'This is Neil, who's a . . . er . . . how do you describe

your act, Neil?' said Matt.

'I'm a body-popper!' said Neil, stepping forward and shaking Barry's hand.

'Hm, well, you'd better pop both your bodies backstage and check everything's to your liking. I'll MC the gig. My wife Tanya's going to sing a couple of hits from the films, then we'll bring young Neil on and then the floor's yours, Matt. After that there'll be the usual disco. To be honest, that's what most of 'em come for. A chance for a bit of a boogie.'

At that point there was a rumbling noise and the hoot of a horn. The assembled group all turned round to see a big coach making its way up the drive to the hotel. As it came to a halt a couple of yards from them the door swung open, revealing a man dressed as a penguin holding a half-empty bottle of beer.

'Is this the right place for the comedy night?' he said.

'That's right,' said Barry. 'Who are you?'

'I'm Pingu!' said the penguin. He then promptly

fell down the steps of the bus and landed in a crumpled heap on the floor, still clutching his bottle of beer. 'Cheers!' he said, taking a swig from the bottle. He staggered to his feet and shouted at the top of his voice, 'Come on, boys! Stag party starts here!'

Out from the coach piled twelve very drunk men, all in various outrageous fancy-dress outfits and clutching half-drunk bottles of beer. As they half walked, half fell up the steps to the hotel past Matt, Neil, Barry and Kitty, they broke out into a bawdy rugby song, peppered with four-letter words.

Matt put his hands over Neil's ears to protect him.

'Hmm,' said Barry. 'Things have just started to get very interesting!'

31

The Gig from Hell

Barry wasn't really cut out to be an MC. His idea of warming the crowd up was to get them all singing 'The Hokey Cokey'. That might have worked at a children's party but at the Cavendish Hotel it only served to encourage the audience to think they could be a part of the show. Add to that the high alcohol content of the stag party and no matter how well the room was laid out or how good the lights and sound were (and they were good – Kitty had made sure of that) the odds were always going to be stacked against any form of entertainment other than the disco.

Barry's wife Tanya was on first. She was a nice lady

with a reasonable voice but as she stepped on to the stage there were wolf whistles and catcalls and shout-outs. She was shocked and as she sang a livid red rash crept up her neck and quickly enveloped most of her face. The taunts didn't let up. She'd planned to sing five numbers, with another held in reserve for a possible encore. She ended up singing one and a half before Barry stepped in to save her.

'Now, gents!' he shouted over the ensuing hullabaloo. 'Can you please show a little respect to the acts tonight and allow them to be heard? I don't mind you heckling me . . .'

'Get lost then!' shouted a man dressed as an orc, from deep within the safety of the stag party.

'Thank you for that!' said Barry. He was sweating heavily now and it was clear to anyone watching that he was no longer in charge of the night, if indeed he'd ever been.

'This is just awful, isn't it?' said a frightened Neil, who was standing at the back of the gig with Matt and Kitty.

'Just focus on your moves and don't let them see you're scared,' said Kitty.

'Yeah, you'll be fine,' said Matt. 'At least you've got music to drown out the heckles!'

At that Kitty walked over to the sound desk, leant in to the sound man and said, 'Turn it up loud!' Matt watched as he slid the fader up to max.

'Ladies and gentlemen, please welcome the body-popping styles of Neil Trottman!'

'We must do something about that name,' muttered Kitty.

'Here, hold these!' said Neil, handing Matt his bow tie and boater and starting out towards the stage.

As the music began the crowd immediately started clapping along and stamping their feet. Neil started his moves, but he had a look in his eyes that Matt could see, even from the back of the room, was fear. Where previously his dancing had been loose, instinctive and infectiously joyous, it was now tight and automatic. He was getting through it, though, and it looked to Matt like he might get away with it. Then Pingu ran up on to the stage and joined him.

Neil soldiered on but it wasn't easy with a grown man dressed as a penguin, pulling faces, falling over and completely disrupting his routine. The audience was in hysterics – but for all the wrong reasons. Matt would have been laughing too if he hadn't been so worried about his own act. He started to flick through his little black book, looking for heckle put-downs. Neil quickly lost his place, tried a bit of jogging on the spot to fill the time and amazingly managed to end on the splits. He came off to a huge commotion of jeers and cheers and applause. Pingu meanwhile stayed on and took several bows, then took the mic and tried to sing before Barry managed to wrestle it from him and get him to sit back down. It was bedlam.

Poor Neil was close to tears as he made his way back to join Matt and Kitty. As he got close his mum swept him up in a big hug and took him out to the hotel restaurant with the promise of an ice cream.

'Wow!' thought Matt. 'That was hardcore!' He'd always thought Neil's act was bulletproof. If Neil had bombed how the hell was he going to fare? 'They're going to have me for breakfast!' he said to Kitty. 'What should I do?'

'Um ...' It was the first time Matt had ever seen Kitty Hope lost for words. 'Focus on your set ... er ... don't let them see you're scared ...' she said limply.

'Yeah, cos that worked for Neil, right?' he said.

Meanwhile onstage Barry was trying once again to settle the audience down, only this time he'd given up on any idea of subtlety. 'FOR CRYING OUT LOUD JUST SHUT UUUUUP!' he bellowed into the mic. The audience were stunned into silence – for about ten seconds, then started up even louder.

Before Matt could catch his breath or make a plan he heard Barry announcing his name.

'Please welcome a young comic by the name of Matt Millz!'

Matt set off from the back of the room on what seemed like a very long journey to the stage, fighting his way through the rowdy crowd all the way. As he got there he grabbed the mic, but before he could open his mouth to speak, one of the stags shouted, 'Does your mum know you're out this late?!' to a big laugh from his cronies.

Matt remembered Kitty's words and feigned a knowing laugh like this was just water off a duck's back.

'Yeah, I was the same after my first pint!' he said, pleased with himself for remembering one of his list of stock heckle put-downs.

'Not one pint, mate,' shouted the heckler. 'Eight!' Another raucous laugh.

Hmm, it hadn't said on the website what to say when the heckler came back at you. Matt hesitated for a moment.

'Taxi for Matt Millz!' shouted the heckler, then, seizing his moment, started singing the chant favoured by rugby clubs all over Britain. 'Swiiiiiiiing looooooooow, sweeeeeeeet chaaaaariot!' and before long not just the stags but the entire room were singing along with him. Matt felt paralysed, rooted to the spot like a rabbit caught in the headlights of a truck. Nothing that he'd read or seen or heard from Kitty had prepared him for this. He'd completely lost control of the audience. They were now a huge, untamed beast that was writhing about and eating everything before it! As Matt stood, open-mouthed, staring at them, he realised the tables had been turned. THEY were now the performer and he had become THE AUDIENCE. He knew when he was beat. He quietly returned the microphone to its stand and slunk off. It was only when Barry announced the disco a couple of minutes later that they even realised he'd gone.

Matt stumbled out on to the steps of the hotel, where just an hour earlier he'd arrived with his heart full of hope, and gulped in the cool night air. He felt sick to the pit of his stomach with shame. He'd let everybody down, including himself. How could something he'd worked so hard for vanish into thin air like that?

'Never mind, I'm sure your next one will go better.' It was Mr Gillingham.

'Thanks, sir.'

'Need a lift home?'

'No thanks, I'm fine, Neil's mum's giving me a lift.'

He felt an arm round his shoulders.

'Don't know what to say, mate!' It was Rob. 'Even Eddie Odillo would have struggled with that crowd.'

'I thought you were very . . . er . . . brave! Yes, very brave!' said Magda awkwardly, looking as lovely as ever.

'You died, bruv!' said Ahmed, coming up behind them. 'Pooh, what's that smell? It's a corpse called

Matt Mi—'

Rob gave him a big shove. 'That's enough, Ahmed!' he said. 'C'mon, my dad's waiting. See you tomorrow, Matt.'

As the last few stragglers disappeared into the night Matt looked up at a moth divebombing the lamp hanging in the doorway above him. He felt just like that moth, vainly throwing himself at something he could never attain, and hurting himself in the process.

'I should have thrown them out!' came a voice behind him. It was Barry. 'They ruined it for everyone.'

Matt shrugged, still studying the moth as it attacked the lamp in ever more desperate swoops.

'No, that wouldn't have been fair. They paid their money like everybody else,' said Kitty, joining them with Neil in tow. She reached up and placed a comforting hand on Matt's shoulder. He shrugged it off. Barry turned and padded back to the bar.

'So, Kitty, what should I have done differently?'

said Matt, spinning round to face her.

She paused, a kind of lost look in her eyes.

'I don't know, Matt. Sorry, I wish I did, but I just don't know.'

'But you're my manager . . .'

'I'm eleven. I've only been to two gigs, this one and "Anglebrook's Got Talent"!'

'But what if something like this happens tomorrow night?' said Matt. 'What do I do then, when I'm in front of ten million TV viewers?'

'I'm sorry but I don't have an answer to that question.'

She looked at her feet just as the moth fell lifeless to the floor.

32

Unlucky for Some

There was a huge crowd of people of all shapes and sizes outside the Apollo as Matt and Kitty walked up to those familiar brass-handled doors.

'Who are all these people?' asked Matt, looking round in wonderment.

'That's your audience, Matt!'

'Jeez! There's millions of 'em!'

'Three thousand six hundred . . .' said Kitty.

'. . . and thirty-two,' said Matt. 'Yeah, you told me!' All the colour had drained from his face. 'I'm a goner!' he thought to himself.

'Everything OK?' asked Kitty, noticing his rather queasy appearance.

'Yup!' said Matt. 'The more the merrier!'

'Audience or contestant?' asked a burly bouncer as they pushed to the front of the barriers.

'Contestant,' said Matt with a gulp.

'Thought so,' said the bouncer. 'I can usually tell – the contestants are the ones that look like they've just seen a ghost. You need to go round the back to the stage door. Someone will show you where to go from there.'

As they set off towards the stage door there was a massive cheer and the crowd surged forwards. Matt looked round to see three immaculate black Rolls-Royce saloon cars sweeping round the front of the building, heading towards the stage door.

'Talking of Phantoms . . .' said the bouncer archly.

The cars stopped and one by one discharged their precious cargo. They were the famous *T Factor* judges – Simon Bewell, David Wallnuts and Amanda Thrustup, or, as they were known on the show, Mr Nasty, Mr Funny and Mrs Nice. They'd been household names for almost ten years. With a few limp waves they disappeared into the building and Matt and Kitty headed after them.

At the stage door they were each given a *T Factor* 'Performer' wristband and met by a production runner dressed in a black T-shirt emblazoned with the *T Factor* logo.

'Matt Millz?' said the runner, checking Matt's name off against her list. She gave him a puzzled look. 'You know the minimum age is sixteen, don't you, Matt?'

'Yes, he turned sixteen last Wednesday. He just looks young for his age,' said Kitty, taking over.

'And you are . . . ?'

'Kitty Hope, I'm his manager.'

'Oh, right. You, er, both look young for your age then . . . right . . . You're lucky, you've got a dressing room to yourself. Follow me.'

The production runner led them up a series of stairs and corridors right up to the top of the building.

'I hope you're remembering the route, Kit,' said Matt. 'I'll never find my way back from here.'

'You won't need to,' said the runner. 'We need you to stay put in the dressing room until you're called.'

'Where is Matt on the running order?' asked Kitty.

'Um, let me see ...' said the runner, flicking through some paperwork. 'Not till the second half, so you've got plenty of time – about an hour and a half if it all runs smoothly.'

'Great!' thought Matt – he really needed some time alone to go through his set list.

'Here we are, dressing room 13.'

'Unlucky for some,' said Matt gloomily.

'You'll be fine!' said the runner brightly. 'Just try to enjoy it! If you need anything here's my number, give me a call – but try not to wander about too much, because if I lose you, I lose my job. Any questions?'

'Just one,' said Matt. 'Where's the loo?'

'Ha!' laughed the runner. 'Down the corridor, first on your left. I'll leave you to it. See you in just over an hour.'

Matt put his sports bag on the dressing-room table and flicked the light switch. Immediately about fifty light bulbs lit up around the mirror stretching the length of the table. 'Dah da-da da-da da daaaaah!' Matt hummed the song 'There's No Business like Showbusiness'.

'There certainly isn't!' said Kitty.

Matt fished out a tattered piece of paper from his sports bag. 'The Holy Grail!' he said reverently. 'My set list!'

T Factor Set List

DON'T FORGET TONGUE

· Simon's hair

· So Young stuff — Rusk/Mum picks
me up after gigs/ Can't go last
(bedtime)

· Voucher for Mothercare

- BUT still not young enough for Amanda (face lift)

- David Wallnuts stuff (marriage breakup)

- T Factor highlights (screaming woman, gets through cos of backstory - her dad's ill)

- My fake backstory (dog got diarrhoea Mum cold sore/guinea pig with asthma)

- Voting face

- Nan mix-ups (hair caught in knitting)

- From small town (electric lights/ twinned with itself/ town motto)

There was a small speaker mounted on the wall that relayed all the action from the stage. They could hear the warm-up man trying to make the audience laugh. The show was about to start.

'Is there any way to turn that off?' said Matt anxiously. 'It's making me nervous.'

Kitty reached an experienced hand up to the volume knob on the side of the speaker and turned the sound right down.

'You seem to know this place pretty well,' observed Matt.

'Yes, I used to come up quite a lot when Grandpa had an office here,' she said.

'Ah yes, the great Bernie Hopestein!' said Matt. 'Respect due.'

'In fact, if my memory serves me correctly his

office was on the floor above this one. Shall we see if we can find it?'

'Well, that lady told us to stay put, but yeah, I could do with stretching my legs. It might calm me down a bit.'

'We just need to keep an eye on the time, that's all,' said Kitty. She pulled the dressing-room door open and wandered off down the painted brick corridor with Matt close behind.

33

History

They walked a little way, then through a door, up some stairs, and came to another door with 'NO ENTRY' written on it. Kitty looked at Matt, then turned the handle. It turned easily and before they knew it they were in another corridor that was thick with dust and rubbish and generally looked like no one had walked along it for years.

'Hey, Kitty! Look at this!' said Matt, taking his hanky out and rubbing a layer of dust from a brass plate attached to a closed door. Kitty joined him. Under the dust was a name engraved in capital letters:

SIR BERNARD HOPESTEIN
Managing Director

'This is it!' she said and tried the door handle. It wouldn't budge at first but with a little bit of a wiggle and a big push from Matt it jolted open and the two of them walked inside. The office looked like a bomb had hit it. There were chairs strewn higgledy-piggledy around the wood-panelled room. In the centre was a large oak desk with an old-fashioned anglepoise light on it and next to it a metal filing cabinet. The floor was strewn with piles of ancient paperwork. The whole lot was covered in a thick layer of dust – it obviously hadn't been touched for years. Matt looked at Kitty, mouth agape in wonder.

'Untidy bloke, your grandpa, wasn't he?' he said with a smirk.

'Actually he was one of the most organised people I've ever met,' said Kitty. 'He'd be furious if he could see this now!'

'I thought I told you two to keep out?!' came a gruff voice from behind them. It was the old gent who'd delivered them down the steps of the Apollo just two days earlier.

'Sorry, Mr Bramble,' said Matt, wishing he was back in his dressing room and concentrating on his act. 'How's your wife?'

'Never mind that!' snapped the old gent. 'In Mr Hopestein's office too.'

'Tell him, Kitty,' said Matt, but Kitty hesitated.

'Tell me what?' said Mr Bramble.

'She's Kitty Hope, Bernie's granddaughter.'

'Say again?' said Mr Bramble.

'He's right. I'm Kitty Hope. My parents shortened our surname from Hopestein because they got fed up with people asking if we were related to Bernie.'

'Really?!' said Wilfred, his face cracking into a broad grin.

Kitty nodded.

'Ha!' he exclaimed, grabbing both of Kitty's hands. 'The last time I saw you you were about so high!' he said, holding his hand out about two and a half feet above the ground.

'Not quite the last time,' said Kitty.

'I didn't know it was possible for her to be any smaller than she is now!' joked Matt.

'Fancy me throwing out the guv'nor's grand-daughter – he'd have had my uniform for that. Why didn't you tell me? I would have given you a tour!'

'Rather than booting us down the front steps?' muttered Matt.

'I don't like to trade on Grandpa's name, Wilfred. I'm determined to make my own way in the world.'

'Well, good for you,' said Wilfred. 'What are you up to? You here for this awful talent thingy?'

'I'm a comedian – Matt Millz,' said Matt, shaking Wilfred by the hand. 'And she's my manager.'

'Ah! It's in the blood!' said Wilfred, clapping his hands together excitedly. 'The old man would have been proud of you! Of course, this is where it all happened, where your grandfather controlled his empire! Literally – the Finsbury Park Empire, the Hackney Empire, the Chiswick Empire … in fact, most of the big theatres in London!'

'He must have been quite something,' said Matt.

'Oh, he was a great man. Above all he believed in talent – that it should be looked after and nurtured. He must be turning in his grave at this *T Factor* thing – a career in showbiz takes more than a two-minute spot on the TV.'

'Well, times have changed, Wilfred,' said Kitty.

'Yes and not for the better,' said Wilfred. 'There are so many memories in this place. Don't get me wrong, your grandpa had quite a temper on him when pushed – firm but fair, that was him – but he never forgot that show business should be fun and not just about profits. I can remember him saying to me that we should never forget, us "show people" as he called us, that most people are stuck working in some office somewhere in a job they don't like just to pay the bills, and that us lot – we lucky few who ran away and joined the circus – we'd escaped the rat race. I've never forgotten that. Yes, he was a good sort, the best.'

'There you are! I've been looking for you everywhere!' It was the production runner and she seemed a little bit annoyed. 'I thought I told you to stay in your dressing room!'

'Hey!' said Wilfred. 'You can't talk to her like that, she's . . .'

But before he could finish, the runner delivered her bombshell. 'I've been trying to find you because there's been a change in the running order. One of the other acts has fallen ill so you're taking his place.'

'You mean . . . ?'

'Yes. You're on!'

34

The Big Gig

'Dead man walking,' muttered Matt two minutes later as he followed the production runner out of his dressing room and down the warren of busy backstage corridors. There were people in black *T Factor* T-shirts darting about, carrying cameras, lights and odd bits of scenery, and then there were the other acts. Matt glanced into dressing rooms as he passed them: a street-dance group packed into one like sardines, a ventriloquist sat talking to a stuffed parrot in another, a lady in a cowboy hat with a troupe of chihuahuas, singers, breakdancers . . . this, in short, was show business in all its glorious variety.

He could hear the show getting louder as he and
Kitty got closer to the stage. Then they turned a
corner, walked through some black drapes and they
were upon it.

'All right mate?'

Matt looked up to see *T Factor* hosts Titch and
Tot.

'Er, yes, I think so anyway,' he said, a little star-struck. He'd been watching these two guys since he was five!

'Nothing to be nervous about,' said Titch. (Or was it Tot? Matt could never remember which was which.)

'Just go out there and do your best, mate!' said the other one.

On stage was an elderly man attempting to juggle some plates. Matt couldn't get a clear view of it from the wings but judging by the sound of breaking crockery it wasn't going too well. Finally there was a huge crashing sound and the old man finished up to a smattering of polite applause.

'Hmm, maybe next time instead of plates try juggling balloons – it might be safer!' came a voice which Matt instantly recognised as belonging to David Wallnuts.

There was a big laugh, and then in time-honoured fashion one by one the judges gave the old chap their verdicts.

'That's three Nos, I'm afraid, Freddie – sorry,

mate, don't give up the day job,' said Simon.

'I haven't got a day job!' said Freddie, gathering up the broken plates and shuffling off. 'Good luck with that bunch,' he said as he shuffled past Matt and Kitty. 'Tough crowd!'

'OK, time to go, Matt.' It was the production runner again. 'Remember, walk straight out to the middle spot and talk into the microphone. Any questions?'

Matt's mind was completely blank. How had he got here? In a few short weeks he'd gone from his first ever gig in a school talent show to playing a packed house at the Hammersmith Apollo. He looked at Kitty.

'What if it goes like last night?'

'It won't. Sometimes you need a bad one before you have a good one,' she said, trying to sound confident, but in truth she looked more nervous than he did.

He raised his eyebrows as if to say 'Now?'

Kitty nodded. 'Don't forget the tongue. Break a leg!' she whispered.

He took a deep breath and walked out into the spotlight, his mouth open and his tongue dangling out.

As he got to the mic he did a double take at the judges, just like he'd seen Laurel and Hardy do on the DVD, then pushed his tongue back into his mouth with his finger. There was a ripple of laughter. Simon glanced across at David and they exchanged a look.

'What's your name?' said Simon.

'Matt Millz,' said Matt, his voice cracking as he leant in to the microphone. The volume of his reply startled him and he immediately recoiled from the mic.

'Hi, Matt,' continued Simon. 'Tell us why you want to win *The T Factor*.'

Matt shifted uneasily. He'd known this question was likely to come up but he still hadn't thought of a satisfactorily pithy answer. So he decided to tell the truth.

'I just love making people laugh, Simon. I dunno, it just makes me feel good.'

There was a cry of 'Alriiiight!' from high up in the dress circle that Matt thought he recognised. Simon turned to acknowledge the heckle.

'Well,' he said, 'someone likes you!'

'Have you got any family with you, Matt?' This time it was Amanda.

'No, no, they don't know I'm here. I've just got my ...' He hesitated and glanced into the wings, where he could see a very worried Kitty standing with her clipboard and stopwatch. 'My manager – Kitty, Kitty Hope.'

'Kitty!' called David Wallnuts. 'We want to meet you! Come on out!'

There was a pause. Matt could see Titch and Tot trying to talk Kitty into joining him on stage. Then there was a massive 'Ahhhhhh!' as the eleven-year-old girl in glasses finally relented and walked out to join him.

'Aw! She's so cute!' squealed Amanda.

'So you think your boy can win, do you?' said Simon with a wry smile.

Kitty spoke but no one could hear it. Matt bent down, put his arms around her waist and lifted her up to the microphone.

'I think Matt's got real talent, Simon, and I honestly believe he could win this competition.'

Once again the audience swooned.

'I wish my manager was as positive about my talents!' joked David.

Matt eased her gently down to the ground. 'Nice one!' he whispered.

Kitty walked briskly back to the side of the stage. Matt could see Titch and Tot high-fiving her as she reached them.

'Right then,' said Simon. 'You've got a lot to prove, young man – off you go!'

There was a lighting change. Matt stepped forward to the microphone, took it off its stand and started.

'Thanks, Simon. Simon Bewell, ladies and gentleman – the only person in show business who has his hair dry-cleaned . . .'

As Matt finished the line something extraordinary

happened – the audience laughed. Not just a little laugh or even a big laugh like the ones he and Rob had got at the school talent show, no, this was something of a completely different order. It was like a shockwave. In fact, as it hit him it all but took his breath away. Matt staggered back slightly, winded. He gulped for air. The room started spinning. He grabbed the microphone stand to steady himself and somehow managed to get out his next gag.

'I know a lot of you are looking at me thinking, "Blimey, he's young." It's true, I'm so young that if I'm having a drink I still like to have a rusk with it!'

Another shockwave of laughter hit him in the chest but this one didn't knock him back, no, this time something inside him kicked in. Instinct. Matt didn't understand how he knew how long to let each laugh start to die down before throwing out his next gag, he didn't know why within a couple of seconds he was prowling the stage like a tiger, he couldn't tell you how he knew to turn at certain points, to deliver punchlines in particular places, to pull faces or illustrate his gags with actions. It just happened. Unlike the WI gig where he'd had just a few moments to judge whether to embellish the lines with a look or an ad lib, here the laughs bought him thinking time. Sometimes he'd let the laugh die away completely to build a little tension – then POW! In with the killer punchline. Other times he'd hit them with three gags in quick succession, POW! POW! POW! He felt something he hadn't really experienced before as a twelve-year-old boy. He felt powerful, like he was controlling this huge crowd – dragging them this way and that to wherever he wanted them to go. He could see people rocking back and forth in their seats. One middle-aged lady in the front row had tears streaming down her face. He almost wanted to turn round to see if someone else had come on – surely they couldn't possibly be laughing at him? But they were. And most importantly of all, so were the judges – even Simon was chuckling away self-consciously, exchanging looks with David.

The only person not laughing was Kitty Hope. No, she was standing in the wings watching Matt with a look of absolute concentration. 'Come on, that's it, take your time . . .' she muttered to herself, like a trainer sitting ringside at a boxing match.

And the laughs kept building and building until there was nothing left for Matt to do but get off.

'My name's Matt Millz, that's all from me – goodnight!' he hollered over the laughter and with a slight bow of the head stepped back from the mic. The whole place erupted – 3,632 pairs of hands clapped wildly. Matt wasn't ready for the emotions that the audience reaction sparked in him – it was almost too much, overwhelming. That five minutes had seemed like thirty seconds. He was laughing, yet he felt like crying. He looked to the wings and saw Kitty jumping up and down and clapping and screaming – he'd never seen her so animated!

It was David Wallnuts who spoke first. 'That was really funny, Matt, unbelievably accomplished for someone so young. Well done!'

'Oh you're so cute, Matt!' squealed Amanda. 'I just love you! I want to take you home with me!'

'Not sure you should take her up on that offer, Matt,' said Simon drily, then gave his assessment. 'Look, Matt, I don't usually like comedians, but you're young, you came out here and you made a couple of thousand people laugh. Fair play to you. I think you've got a big future in this business. Right! Let's vote!'

Matt closed his eyes and allowed himself a moment to think back over the last couple of weeks. The 'Anglebrook's Got Talent' show, the run-ins with Mr Pavey, the ill-fated gig for the ladies of the WI, the ups and downs with his best friend Rob, teaming up with Kitty, being chucked out of the Apollo on their first trip, Mrs Trottman's and Magda's makeover, and hitting rock bottom with the awful gig at the Cavendish, just last night. Wow! He'd heard people on talent shows describe their 'journey' as being 'a roller-coaster ride' a thousand times, but now there seemed no phrase that came closer to pinning it down. It had been a ride all right, the ride of his life!

As he stood there with his eyes closed he was suddenly aware that the judges were taking an awfully long time to make their decisions.

He opened his eyes.

One of the production assistants was talking animatedly to Simon, who looked suddenly very serious.

'Hang on a sec,' said Simon. He whispered something to Amanda, who pulled a face, then he looked at Matt. Then another man arrived, who Matt recognised as the show's producer.

Matt looked nervously into the wings and shrugged at Kitty. She shrugged back – neither of them knew what was going on. All Matt could do was stand there like a spare part and wait.

The audience started to get restless, muttering to one another. One or two got up to stretch their legs.

Finally the producer stepped to one side and Simon turned to face Matt.

'How old are you, Matt?' he said softly.

'I'm sixtee—' Then he checked himself. 'I'm twelve, Simon,' he said, looking at the shiny black floor. He couldn't lie, not to all those people.

There was a gasp from the crowd, then a shout of, 'Let him go through!' Someone else called out, 'Three yesses!' Then the whole crowd started chanting, 'YES! YES! YES!'

Simon held up his hand and the chanting stopped as quickly as it had started.

'Listen, Matt, if it was up to me I'd put you through, but you know the rules. Even I can't bend them for one person, however special or talented that person might be. I'm afraid you're out.' There was a huge groan from the audience and Simon added, 'Come back in four years.'

The house lights came up in the theatre, the judges stood to leave and the warm-up man came straight on. 'Right, folks, bit of a hiccup there, we're going to take a five-minute break. Don't go away!'

Matt felt stunned and bewildered as the audience all shuffled around and started talking. The theatre seemed to close in on him now. The audience noise became a deep, low rumble. Things seemed to be moving in slo-mo. How could he have got so close to his dream only for it to be snatched away at the last minute? He felt slightly sick, slightly choked up, and then something else kicked in. Anger. How could Kitty have let this happen? He'd told her he was too young, she knew he had next to no stand-up experience – he'd only really done two gigs as a solo act and both times he'd bombed. What on earth had she been thinking, booking him on to the biggest show on TV?

He felt a hand on his elbow.

'Come on, Matt, you need to leave now.' It was the same runner who'd looked after him before the show.

'Yeah, sorry,' he said, shaking his head, trying to snap out of the funk that was enveloping him. He took one last look at the auditorium, then turned and walked towards Kitty in the wings.

He expected to see the same serious face that he was wearing but instead she was beaming from ear to ear. 'You did it! You did it, Matt!' she squealed excitedly.

'What are you talking about, Kit? I got disqualified!'

'I knew you would!'

'What?!' he snapped, the angry feeling all but bubbling over.

'I knew there was no way you'd get away with it, but don't you see?' she continued. 'You made all those people laugh! You smashed it! You knocked them dead! And you know what, this is a much better story!'

'Better story?' said Matt, his anger turning to confusion.

'Yes! The winners of these shows never go on to do much. Nine times out of ten they're a flash in the pan, one-hit wonders. I bet you can't name last year's *T Factor* winner.'

Matt hesitated. 'Er . . . was it that piano-playing parrot?'

'Beethoven the Budgie was two years ago!' she laughed.

'The big bloke with the teeth who sang opera whilst standing on his head?'

'Peter Price was five years ago! You can bet your life the papers will be all over this tomorrow – don't you see? You're the one that got away!'

'She's right.' It was Titch. (Or was it Tot?) '*We* can't even remember who won last year and we present the show!' said the other one. 'You did really well out there!'

It started to dawn on Matt exactly what they were both getting at.

'The fact that you're twelve is even more impressive. You're the youngest stand-up to raise the roof at the Apollo!' said Kitty.

'Yeah, I suppose you're right,' said Matt with

a chuckle. 'Yeah, I'm the winner that didn't win!'

'Exactly!' said Kitty.

'There's some people here say they're friends of yours?' It was the bouncer from earlier. Matt looked past him to see Mr Gillingham, Ahmed, Neil Trottman and what looked like the entire school.

'What are you doing here?' asked Matt in disbelief, a big lump forming in his throat.

'We didn't want to miss your big break!' said Mr Gillingham. 'Your ex double act partner tipped me off, so I was told to organise a coach by your number one fan.'

'Number one fan?' said Matt.

'Come on out!' said Mr Gillingham.

'I don't believe it!' said Matt, running a hand through his hair, because behind Mr G was the headmaster himself, Mr Pavey.

'Bravo, Matt! I very much enjoyed your set. That is to say, I would have liked a few more jokes about the WI, but . . .'

'Thanks for coming, Mr P!' said Matt.

'I wouldn't have missed it for the world.'

'Matty!' came a shrill voice from behind them. He recognised it straight away, of course – only one person had the nerve to call him Matty in public. Matt turned and sure enough, it was his mum, in a big fake-fur coat and hat, dragging a wheelie suitcase behind her.

'Darling, that was amazing!' she gushed. 'I'm gobsmacked! Lost for words!'

'That'll be a first then,' said Ian, popping up behind her with the rest of her luggage.

'I don't understand – where did all that come from?' she said, planting a big wet kiss on his forehead.

'I dunno, Mum, it's just something I've been wanting to do for a long time.'

He gave his mum a hug. It was really good to see her – even if she did smell strongly of dog food. As he hugged her Matt heard a strange yelping sound that seemed to be coming from under her armpits.

'Oops!' she said, and reaching inside her coat she

produced two miniature dachshunds. 'Sorry about the dogs, I came straight from the station.'

'Very pleased to meet you, Mr and Mrs Mills!' It was Kitty, beaming with pride. 'You must be very proud, sir,' she said to Ian.

'Er . . .' Ian hesitated then swallowed hard. 'Yes, Kitty, I am as a matter of fact. I'm extremely proud! All that hard work paid off!'

'I don't get it. How did Rob know about the gig?' said Matt.

'Magda told us!' It was his old mate Rob Brown, pushing through the throng with Magda Avery, and what's more, they appeared to be holding hands.

'Well, I reckoned you could do with some support,' she said.

'This is like an episode of *This Is Your Life!*' laughed Matt. 'So you two are . . . an item?' he added, raising an inquisitive eyebrow.

'You don't mind, do you?' said Rob sheepishly. 'We've been spending a lot of time together . . . what with the portrait . . . and you've been busy, so . . .'

'Mind?' said Matt, looking at the two of them. He couldn't deny he felt a slight pang of jealousy. He quickly weighed the options up in his head. Which would he prefer? What he'd just done on *The T Factor* or winning Magda Avery's heart? No contest, it had to be *The T Factor* every time. 'I'm cool with it,' he said magnanimously – like he had a choice. 'But it's Dave Joy you need to look out for, isn't it?'

'He's in hospital,' said Rob.

'I did warn him, bruv!' said Ahmed, pushing through the crowd to congratulate Matt. 'Didn't I tell him about the danger of motorcycles?'

'Nah!' said Magda, giving Ahmed a friendly shove. 'He didn't come off his motorbike, he dropped one of his drums on his foot and broke it!'

'Which sadly makes the prospect of a Toxic Cabbage reunion even more distant,' opined Mr G.

'The world of music is in mourning today, as the

drummer of hit rock band Toxic Cabbage has been taken to hospital with a broken foot,' said Matt, putting on his best serious news reporter voice. 'We go now to our music correspondent, Rob Brown, who assesses their impact on the world of rock.'

'Thank you, Matt,' said Rob, picking up his cue. 'Thousands of fans ... well, two ... well, Dave's mum and dad ... are staging an all-night vigil at the stricken Toxic Cabbage drummer's bedside.'

'No, don't be mean, you two!' said Magda, trying not to laugh. 'Poor Dave.'

'Yeah, we're completely stuck without a drummer.' It was the lead singer of Toxic Cabbage, Freddie Metcalfe. 'We were s'posed to 'ave a gig next week at the 'orse and Groom.'

'Ahem!' coughed Ian and dug Matt sharply in his ribs with his elbow. Matt looked at Ian, then it dawned on him.

'I know a drummer that could sit in for you!'

'Yeah?' said Freddie.

'Yeah, Ian here!'

'Really?' said Freddie. 'He looks a bit old. No offence, mate. Is he any good?'

'I'd say, judging by what I've heard from both of you,' said Matt, 'he's at exactly the right level.'

'Deal!' said Freddie Metcalfe, shaking Ian's hand.

'Deal!' said Ian, punching the air. 'YES! I'm back!'

'Nice dogs, Mrs M!' It was Simon Bewell. He put out a hand to pat Baron von Munchausen, who promptly tried to bite him. 'Sorry about how it all worked out, Matt. I tried my best but rules is rules, I'm afraid. If you're ever looking for management give me a call,' he said, holding out his business card.

'Thanks for the offer, Simon, but I think the manager I've got at the moment is doing a pretty good job.'

'Actually, Matt, I think you're right,' said Simon, smiling at Kitty and returning the card to his jacket pocket. 'Good luck, and see you in a few more years, I hope,' he said and headed out of the stage door to his waiting limo.

Magda whooped loudly and followed Simon with a couple of the other girls in search of a selfie.

'Wow! Matt Millz!' came a voice that Matt thought he recognised.

It couldn't be – could it?

Matt turned round and there he was – tall, dark, his black hair cropped close to his scalp, and dressed in his trademark electric-blue mohair suit – Matt's hero, Eddie Odillo.

'That was very funny. How long you been doing it?' he said, shaking Matt by the hand.

'Erm . . . I . . .' Matt was having difficulty catching his breath. 'I . . . I am such a . . . big . . . fan of . . . yours!'

'Great!' said Eddie. 'Well, now I'm a fan of yours. We do a show here you may have heard of, *Stand-up at the Apollo*?'

'Yes, I know!' said Matt. 'I never watch it! Sorry, I mean I always miss it!'

'He means he never misses it,' interjected Rob. 'We both love it.'

'Well, maybe you'd like to come along to a live

recording some time?' Eddie said, handing Matt a business card. 'Here's the number of my PA. Give her a call and she'll arrange it.'

'Sure, Eddie, thanks!' said Matt, taking the card, his face a picture of absolute wonder.

'I got a few people I got to talk to, so ... see you around!' said Eddie and with that he was off into the crowd.

'Did that just happen?' said Matt.

'Push your tongue back in again before someone mistakes you for one of your mum's dachshunds,' said Ian.

'You never know who might be in the audience!!!' said Rob, grabbing Matt and shaking his shoulders. 'Eddie Odillo! Eddie Odillo is a fan of YOURS!'

'The all-conquering power of humour!' said Matt. Then he snapped back into the here and now. 'Hang on! I didn't get a photo!'

And suddenly he was there again.

'Oh, I almost forgot!' said Eddie, reappearing with a grin. 'We didn't get a selfie!'

As Matt emerged into the street outside the Apollo his heart was thumping in his chest like a centipede with a hundred wooden legs running the London Marathon. He hardly remembered the coach journey back to Staplefirst. That night he barely slept a wink. His mind raced with ideas for gags, possibilities for sketches, formats for TV shows – panel shows, sitcoms, quizzes and movies. He was so excited that the next day he was walking around in a fog, almost like the whole world had changed. All the time he waiting for the excitement to die, but it never did. No, the excitement stayed with him because he'd discovered the thing he wanted to do with his life, the thing that he was good at, the thing that he loved – he wanted to make people laugh, he wanted to be a stand-up comedian!

That's all from him, for now anyway. Goodnight!